"You're my wife, Victoria. It's legal."

"We were barely married." Victoria was aware her voice was higher pitched than normal. "It was only for a day."

"And a night." Zac's gaze narrowed, and his cleanly sculpted mouth twisted in a sardonic smile as he added, "Don't forget the night, Victoria. Annulment is definitely not an option."

Victoria stared at him, her hand instinctively moving to her gently rounded stomach. As if she *could* forget that night....

She's sexy,
she's successful...
and she's
PREGNANT!

Relax and enjoy our new series in
Harlequin Presents® about spirited women and
gorgeous men, whose passion results in
pregnancies...sometimes unexpected! Of course,
the birth of a baby is always a joyful event, and
we can guarantee that our characters will
become besotted moms and dads—but what
happened in those nine months before?

Share the surprises, emotions, dramas and
suspense as our parents-to-be come to terms
with the prospect of bringing a new little life into
the world. All will discover that the business of
making babies brings with it the most special
love of all....

Look out next month for:

Expectant Mistress by Sara Wood
Harlequin Presents® #2010

HELEN BROOKS

The Baby Secret

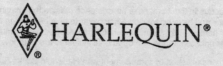

HARLEQUIN®

TORONTO • NEW YORK • LONDON
AMSTERDAM • PARIS • SYDNEY • HAMBURG
STOCKHOLM • ATHENS • TOKYO • MILAN • MADRID
PRAGUE • WARSAW • BUDAPEST • AUCKLAND

ISBN 0-373-12004-4

THE BABY SECRET

First North American Publication 1999.

This edition published by arrangement with Harlequin Books S.A.

® and TM are trademarks of the publisher. Trademarks indicated with ® are registered in the United States Patent and Trademark Office, the Canadian Trade Marks Office and in other countries.

Printed in U.S.A.

CHAPTER ONE

THE doctor's examination was not rough, but Victoria's tenseness still made it uncomfortable and she breathed a sigh of relief when it was over and the little man said, 'You may get dressed now, Miss Brown.'

'Thank you.' She was too taut to smile.

Once seated in front of the doctor's desk, the brilliant Tunisian sun outside the window mocking her gnawing anxiety, the dark-eyed, gentle-faced elderly man stared at her for a few moments before he said, his voice, with its heavy accent, faintly embarrassed, 'Miss Brown, what made you think you were ill?'

Victoria stared back at him, her vivid blue eyes apprehensive as she answered, 'I...I told you. I haven't been feeling too well, sick and dizzy, and lately it's got worse. I've been feeling very tired too, and... Oh, just generally ill. And then when I started to get constant nausea and couldn't keep anything down...'

'Yes, I see.' He cleared his throat loudly and her apprehension increased tenfold. 'Miss Brown, to the best of my knowledge you appear perfectly healthy,' he said quietly, 'but you do realise—?' He stopped abruptly, moving one or two papers on his desk before adding, 'You do understand you are expecting a child?' He raised his dark eyes to her shocked face.

Victoria stared at him, too stunned to react.

'Miss Brown?' The doctor was clearly finding it awkward.

'I'm not... I can't be...' She looked at him in total confusion. '*I can't be,*' she whispered bewilderedly, her eyes huge.

5

'With your permission I would like to do a pregnancy test,' Dr Fenez said gently, 'just to confirm things, but I am sure that I felt a twelve-to-fourteen-week uterus. Now, you say you have only missed one menstrual period?' he asked briskly.

'Yes.' Victoria nodded dazedly. 'Although…'

'Yes?' he asked encouragingly. 'You have thought of something?'

'The last two weren't normal, now I come to think about it. Hardly anything…' She couldn't believe this; he *had* to be wrong.

'That can happen with a first pregnancy—the body takes time to settle into its new role. I take it this *is* your first pregnancy?' he added carefully, his face bland and professional.

Victoria nodded, her mind racing. Pregnancy? Her first *pregnancy*? She had considered various possibilities over the last few weeks, from nervous tension to a growth of some kind, but not this particular kind of growth, she thought with a slight touch of hysteria. She couldn't be; she just couldn't. They had only done it once. That would be too unlucky, wouldn't it?

'Dr Fenez?' She spoke out what was on her mind. 'Can you get pregnant the first time you…?' She waved her hands helplessly.

'Of course.' The little doctor nodded briskly, hiding his concern and surprise at the position this beautiful slender young woman in front of him was in. Not that it was the first time he had come across such a situation—in his long and varied career he had seen many things, especially in the last decade or so as western values had crept into his beloved country—but this girl was different somehow. She hadn't seemed the type. But then there were no types, he reminded himself silently—his own family was proof of that. Look at Kailia, his sister's child—pregnant at sixteen and married within two weeks. His sister had nearly gone mad.

The pregnancy test confirmed the doctor's diagnosis. Victoria was most definitely pregnant, at least three months, the doctor thought, so if she would like to check the date of her last normal period...?

The sun was high in a sapphire-blue sky when Victoria stepped out of the big white-washed building into the fierce heat of a Tunisian summer day, and she stood for a moment, gazing blankly around her, as she tried to gather her scattered wits. She was pregnant. *She was pregnant.* With Zac's child.

She ought to be feeling horrified, upset, desperate, she told herself bewilderedly as she began to walk slowly along the dusty pavement, pulling her big straw hat over her sleek blonde hair as she did so. But she didn't. She just felt amazed, totally astounded...but pleased. She paused, glancing up into the crystal sky as she searched her heart. Yes, she was pleased. She was. This baby would be all that was left of a love that had consumed her with its passion, but it was a million times more than she had dreamt of right up to a few minutes ago. Zac's baby... She didn't realise she was crying until the sun scorched the rivulets running down her cheeks, and then she brushed her face hastily, walking more briskly as she made her way home through the busy, crowded streets.

The little white domed house Victoria was renting was cool and shaded as she stepped through the front door, the mosaic tiles cold beneath her feet as she kicked off her flat leather sandals and padded through to the tiny kitchen at the rear of the property, where all was quiet and tranquil and breathed peace.

When she had first come here all those weeks ago now, she had been like a wounded animal seeking a hiding place in which to lick its wounds, she thought soberly, pouring herself a glass of the home-made lemonade she kept in the fridge. And the quiet little house, with its uncluttered plain interior and horseshoe-shaped stone steps leading down to the small, slightly sunken garden of sun-drenched grass surrounded by eucalyptus, orange and lemon trees and palms and flowering shrubs, had been like balm to her soul. She would have gone mad if she had had to stay in England another day. She would never forget the overwhelming relief she had felt when she had boarded the plane at Heathrow airport.

She drank the refreshingly cold and tart drink straight down and then poured herself another glass, carrying it through into the sitting room and opening the French doors into the garden before she sat down in the old rocking chair at the side of the windows. It was her favourite spot in the fierce heat of the day when even the shaded garden was too hot for her pale English skin, and she had sat for hours staring out into the brightly spangled vista, her mind going over and over the last whirlwind months since Zac Harding had blazed into her life.

She hadn't done that so much in the last few days, she thought now, shifting slightly in the cushioned seat as the cramp-like pain she had been experiencing on and off for the last weeks made itself known. Her mind seemed to have become numb, frozen almost. Perhaps one could only take so much grief and pain without losing one's sanity? Certainly every time she had pictured Zac with Gina she had felt she was going mad.

Zac Harding. She shut her eyes tightly, but still the tall, lean figure was there in front of her. Raven-black hair just touched with grey, dark, glittering eyes set in a handsome, aesthetic face that was all male—he had a presence that was devastating.

She had first seen him across a crowded room—the oldest cliché in the world, she thought with tired wryness—and from the moment their eyes had met she had known she would never meet another man who would stir her the way he did. It wasn't just his smouldering good looks, stunning though they were, or the aura of wealth and power that surrounded him. She would have been able to resist that—she had in the past, hadn't she? She'd come from a privileged background and had known other men just as wealthy and influential as Zac. But he was different. He had a magnetism, a dark, sardonic sensualness that was lethal, and women went down before it like ninepins. She'd gone down before it...

But he had told her she was special. And, fool that she was, she had believed him. Victoria's soft mouth tightened and she opened her eyes wide before shaking her head at her own stupidity. How could she have been so naive, so simple and trusting? she asked herself disgustedly. And it wasn't as if she hadn't been warned either. Everyone had said she was crazy to believe that Zac Harding could ever settle for one woman. And in the final event he hadn't; she had been proved wrong and everyone had been able to nod their wise heads and tut-tut as her world had fallen apart around her ears. The few that knew, that was.

A sharp knock at the front door of the small, two-bedroomed house brought her out of her reverie like a douche of cold water. In the whole of the two months she had been here she had had no visitors, apart from William Howard who was an old and dear friend of hers and who owned the property, and he had popped over on two occasions from England just to make sure she was all right. He had offered her the use of his holiday home in the first dark days of her split with Zac, and she had accepted gratefully, needing desperately to get away from all that was familiar.

It had been a matter of principle that she pay rent for staying at Mimosa—the cottage was so named for the beautiful blossom in the surrounding trees in February and March—but William's parents were due for a visit at the end of June, so Victoria only had another few days in her small sanctuary.

She had been dreading the return home and all it would entail, but now... Victoria's hand rested protectively on her stomach for a brief moment on her way to the front door. Now she had a reason to be strong, a reason to pull herself together and concentrate on the future. And she would do it by herself—she would ask help of no one; she would forge her own destiny and carve out a place for herself and her child. Other women did it—within her own circle there were one or two friends who, by circumstances or design, were both mother and father to their children, but oh… She paused a moment before opening the door. She would have given the world for it not to be this way.

'Hello, Victoria.' Zac's voice was quiet and silky-smooth.

She couldn't move or speak, and she really wondered—for the merest of moments—whether the big dark figure in front of her was a product of her fevered imagination. She had thought about him, dreamt about him, tasted, sensed, *felt* him every single minute of the endless days and nights they had been apart, but the flesh-and-blood man was so much more powerful than her bitter-sweet memories. Devastatingly, frighteningly powerful.

'Can I come in?' He inclined his head towards the sweltering, dusty street behind him. 'It's hot enough to fry eggs out here.'

But still she couldn't respond, and then, as she watched his mouth begin to say something that her ears didn't seem to be able to hear, Victoria knew she was going to pass out. Her last sight of him, as the rushing in her ears became a dark tunnel drawing her down, would have been amusing in any other circumstances. The cool, imperturbable countenance changed, as though someone had flicked a switch, and there was sheer amazement and alarm on his face as he leapt forward to catch her in his arms.

When she came round she was lying on the flamboyantly embroidered sofa in the sitting room, and she opened her eyes to see Zac's angry handsome face just inches from her own as he crouched at her side, his narrowed gaze tight on her.

'You haven't been eating properly.' He was straight into the attack. 'You must have lost a stone in weight.'

It was altogether too much, and Victoria didn't know whether she wanted to laugh or cry. Instead she weakly expostulated, 'What do you expect? I'm a normal human being, Zac; I have annoying things called feelings. *I* can't turn my emotions on and off at will.' She forced the tears back with superhuman effort.

'Meaning I can?' he asked grimly, his lips setting in a hard straight line and his frown ferocious as he eyed her angrily.

But she wasn't going to be intimidated. Not now, not ever, Victoria told herself shakily as she struggled into a sitting position on the sofa and Zac rose to his feet. 'That's exactly what I mean,' she agreed bitterly. And then, as the full horror of the situation dawned on her, she added through trembling lips as her chin rose defiantly, 'And what are you doing here anyway?'

'I was just passing by so I thought I'd call in,' he said, with the cruel, cutting sarcasm he did so well. 'What else?'

'You weren't supposed to know...' Her voice trailed away as the midnight-black eyes blazed at her.

'Where you were hiding?' he finished caustically. 'Oh, I'm fully aware of that, Victoria. No one knows that better than I. I've spent a small fortune trying to find—' He stopped abruptly, taking a long hard pull of air before he said, his formidable composure fully restored and his voice cool, 'Are you feeling better?' He thrust his hands deep into the pockets of his trousers.

'Better?' For a split second she thought he was referring to the baby before she realised how ridiculous she was being. 'Yes, yes, I'm fine now. It's...the heat,' she said quickly.

'Is it?' He glared at her, his dark eyes flashing over her slender shape and pale, drawn face in a razor-sharp scrutiny that did nothing for her fragile equilibrium, before he added insult to injury by stating flatly, 'You look as though a breath of wind would blow you away.' It wasn't meant as a compliment.

'Do I?' She wouldn't have imagined just a few minutes before that she could spring up from the sofa with such suddenness, but the white-hot fury that had her in its grip banished even the faintest remnant of weakness. 'Well, now you've come spreading happiness and cheer, perhaps you'd like to leave? I don't remember inviting you in in the first place,' she added caustically.

'You'd rather I'd left you sprawled in the doorway?' he drawled derisively, his temper apparently quite restored.

'Yes!' And then, as the black eyebrows rose, she amended, 'No. Oh, you know what I mean,' she floundered angrily. 'I was perfectly all right before you came.' She glared at him, her colour high.

'Were you?'

The mockery was all gone, his voice soft and low, and she shivered at its power over her, but her voice was firm when she said, 'I want you to leave, Zac. I want you to leave *now*.'

'I've only just arrived,' he countered easily.

'I mean it.' She raised her chin, looking him full in the face.

'Yes, you probably do.' He looked down at her, the black eyes onyx-hard and very cold. 'But we have things to discuss, Victoria, whether you like it or not.'

'That's where you're wrong.' In the past she had always rather relished the fact that he was nearly ten inches taller than her five feet six inches, but now it was merely daunting. 'I have absolutely nothing to say to you except goodbye,' she said flatly.

'For crying out loud!' It was a snarl of savage frustration. 'What's the matter with you? Listen to me, woman.'

'Don't ''woman'' me, Zac,' Victoria said coldly, forcing her voice to betray none of the trembling that was turning her stomach over and over. 'Save that form of address for—' She found she couldn't say Gina's name and substituted, 'Your other women.'

Part of her couldn't believe she was talking to him like this and she doubted if anyone had before. Zac Harding was a law unto himself, a powerful, ruthless law which was dangerously self-sufficient and utterly without mercy for those who crossed him. He had terrified her when she had first met him all those months ago—terrified and fascinated and enthralled her to the point where she had been unable to imagine a world without him. And then she had thought she didn't have to, she reminded herself painfully. Fool that she was. But she'd learnt her lesson well.

'I refuse to have this conversation again.' It was icy and overbearing, and so utterly *him* that Victoria wanted to stamp her feet and throw a tantrum in a way she hadn't done since she was a toddler. 'And you *will* listen to me, Victoria, but for now—' he eyed her white face and the trembling she couldn't quite hide '—you need something to eat,' he finished smoothly.

'Eat?' She stared at him as though he were mad. 'I don't want anything to eat for goodness' sake, and I've told you—'

'And *I'm* telling you.' He crossed muscled arms over the wide expanse of his chest—a chest that was broad and hairy and wonderful to snuggle up to, Victoria thought weakly, before she slammed the door on that particular avenue of thought—and stood surveying her with narrowed eyes, his legs slightly apart and his body relaxed.

'I've been travelling for I don't know how many hours and I haven't eaten since last night. I'm tired, I'm hungry, and my patience is at an all-time low, okay? Added to which you look as though a good meal would do you no harm at all. Now—' he held up an authoritative hand as Victoria went to speak '—I promise that once we've eaten, and had that little chat, I'll leave.' There was no compromise in his tone.

'I want you to go now,' she repeated stubbornly.

'No way, Victoria.' It was final, and she knew him well enough to know that she could talk until she was blue in the face and they would still end up having that meal.

But she still persisted. 'You've got no right to barge in here like this—' She stopped abruptly as he rounded on her angrily, his dark eyes flashing fire and his face black with rage.

'I have *every* right,' he stated with imperious authority. 'I am your husband—or had that little fact slipped your memory?'

'Only until the divorce becomes final,' she countered swiftly. 'And...and I'm not using my married name any more.'

'That doesn't make you any less married,' he said with unarguable logic. 'You're my wife, Victoria. It's legal.'

'We were barely married.' Victoria was aware her voice was higher-pitched than normal and strived desperately to bring it down an octave or two as she continued, 'It was only for a day.'

'And a night.' His gaze narrowed as he saw his words register in her liquid, violet-blue eyes, his cleanly sculpted mouth twisting in a sardonic smile as he added, 'Don't forget the night, Victoria. Annulment is definitely not an option.'

As if she could forget. She stared at him, her face suffusing with enough colour to satisfy even Zac. She had been an innocent twenty to his experienced and far from innocent thirty-five, and he had taken her into a heaven that was indescribable. The wedding had been a fairy-tale one of white lace and orange blossom, despite the fact that it had all been arranged in as little as four months from the point at which they had got engaged, and every moment had been one of exquisite beauty and romance. But the night... The night had been one of unforgettable passion.

Victoria had been nervous when he had first shut the door of their hotel room, and they were alone at last.

Nervous of her naiveté, of her potential inability to please and satisfy a well-versed man of the world like Zac, of her ingenuousness and lack of sophistication in the arts of love.

She had met Zac Harding the day after she had returned to England from Romania, where she had been taking a year out after A levels working in an orphanage before taking up her university place. She had been nineteen and untouched.

It had been her mother who had introduced them. Coral Chigley-Brown had thrown one of her little parties—ostensibly to celebrate Victoria's safe return from that 'awful place', as her mother termed Romania, but really because Coral was the sort of social butterfly who found a different excuse for a soirée of some kind every week. Even now Victoria could picture the look of satisfaction on her mother's pretty, expertly made-up face as she had watched Zac's dark, glittering eyes narrow with interest on her daughter. She just hadn't known her mother's real reason for desiring an alliance between the Chigley-Browns and the Hardings. Not then.

'Victoria?' Zac's voice brought her back from a dark place. 'I presume this little idyll far from the madding crowd has a kitchen?'

'A kitchen?' She stared at him as though the words were foreign to her and then nodded towards an arched doorway. 'Through there, but if you insist on staying for a meal I'll see to it.'

'Sit down; you look as though you need to,' he said drily. 'I'll sort something out for us.' He eyed her mockingly.

'You?' If he had taken all his clothes off and danced the conga she couldn't have looked more amazed, Zac reflected somewhat cynically. 'You can cook?' Victoria asked weakly.

'Yes, I can cook, Victoria,' he said smoothly. 'I can do a lot of things you are not yet aware of. Now, sit down and think nice thoughts, and once you are looking less drained we can commence battle. Okay?'

He didn't wait for an answer, striding through the doorway into the small kitchen where she heard him beginning to clatter about like an army of chars among William's pots and pans.

She needed to sit down if she were being honest, Victoria thought shakily, staring at the empty doorway one more time before making tremblingly for the rocking chair. It wasn't just that she had skipped breakfast before going to the appointment with the doctor because she had been feeling ill, or the heat and feeling of nausea that were now combining to make her light-headed; it was...it was him, Zac. All her troubles were down to Zac.

He was right when he said there were lots of things she didn't know about him, Victoria thought with painful honesty as she flopped down in the cushioned cane. Their whirlwind courtship and swift marriage had been very much a public affair, and they had hardly been alone at all in the preceding months.

Why hadn't it occurred to her to be suspicious about that? she asked herself now. It was natural for newly engaged couples to want to be alone, surely, but Zac hadn't seemed to want that. But then with Gina in tow, why should he? He'd had everything he wanted.

Lies, lies, lies—their whole relationship had been built on a pack of lies, and it had only been hours after their union that the house of cards had come tumbling down.

Victoria had been vaguely aware of the telephone ringing very early the morning after their wedding, and of Zac reaching out a hand and speaking quietly into the receiver.

She had heard him mutter something into the phone, and then, after sitting up abruptly, he had padded through into the sumptuous sitting room of the bridal suite at the hotel where they had held the reception, and continued the call on the extension in there.

She had still been half awake when he had come back

into the bedroom and begun dressing, and her sleepy, 'Zac, is anything wrong?' had brought a reply of,

'Just a business crisis I need to sort out with Jack before we fly to Jamaica this morning. Go back to sleep, darling, I'll only be a few minutes.'

And, trusting, blind fool that she was, she had gone back to sleep, exhausted by the excitement of the day before and her consuming, wildly passionate and utterly thrilling initiation into the intimacy of married life. Had there ever been such a fool as she?

When she had next surfaced it was to Zac gently kissing her awake, his eyes dark and hot, but when she had held out her arms in an unspoken invitation for him to join her in the massive bed he had shaken his head slowly, softening the refusal with a laughing reminder that they had arranged to share breakfast with the guests who had stayed over at the hotel after the late evening reception. It made her squirm with humiliation now to think of it.

She had felt a little hurt before she'd told herself she was being silly. This was the first day of their lives together as man and wife—they had all the time in the world in which to share their love. But as she had dressed, Zac watching her with a strange expression on his dark, handsome face, Victoria hadn't been able to rid herself of the impression that something was wrong even as she told herself she was being ridiculous.

He hadn't been the adoring, besotted bridegroom of the day before, or the ardent, sensual lover of the night hours, a lover who had tenderly tempered his considerable sexual prowess to her nervous inexperience until she had been as wildly abandoned as he was. He'd been different. Something had changed, and she hadn't been able to put her finger on it. He'd seemed preoccupied.

And then, shockingly, in the elegant, air-conditioned luxury of the hotel lounge, she had discovered why her husband of a few hours had refused her fumbling sexual advances that morning.

Zac had wanted to make a phone call before they went through to join the others for breakfast, and she had sat down in one of the deeply cushioned sofas to wait for him, glancing idly at a glossy magazine and reflecting that she had never imagined it was possible to feel so happy. But she felt *loved*, she'd told herself joyfully. For the first time in her life she felt really loved. Hers had been a privileged childhood in the material sense, but her parents had never made any secret of the fact that they hadn't wanted a child and that she was an intrusion into their lives.

When she had been shipped off to boarding-school at the tender age of seven, it had been her nanny she had cried for—she had barely known her parents. And when her father had died three years later she had attended the funeral of a stranger. As she had gone into her teenage years she had tried to get to know her mother, but after countless cold rebuffs had finally accepted they were a million miles apart in everything that mattered.

Her mother was an avid socialite who used her considerable wealth for a life of pampered luxury, and who worried more about a chip in her nail varnish than starving children in the Third World. Victoria's gentle, sweet nature was anathema to her mother—Coral saw it only as weakness and despised her for it.

And so, as Victoria had sat waiting for her new husband on this, the first morning of her new life, her heart had sunk slightly when that familiar voice had sounded at her elbow, saying, 'Victoria? What on earth are you skulking out here for?'

There had been no real justification in Coral's taking advantage of Zac's generous offer to provide accommodation at the hotel for any guests who wanted to stay over for the night after the celebrations—she only lived a short drive away in a sumptuous apartment in Kensington—but it hadn't surprised Victoria either. Coral was like that. She took everything she could and then some.

'Skulking?' Victoria forced a smile as she turned in her seat to look up at the hard, pretty face staring down at her. 'I'm not skulking, Mother. I'm waiting for Zac,' she said quietly.

'Are you?' Her mother paused, frowning slightly before she said, 'You really ought to get in there with all the others and show them you don't care, Victoria. It's the only way.'

'Don't care?' Victoria echoed confusedly.

'Exactly.' Coral's voice was sharp and impatient.

'Mother, I'm sure this conversation is making sense to you but I don't have a clue what you are on about,' Victoria said patiently. 'What is it I'm not supposed to care about?'

'You mean you don't know?' Coral sank gracefully into a seat opposite her daughter, crossing her legs and raising her chin slightly in order to show her profile to its best advantage to anyone who might be watching. 'I would have thought Zac would have told you by now,' she added disapprovingly, her eyes narrowing on Victoria's beautiful, slightly bewildered face. It was a source of constant aggravation to Coral that such beauty had been wasted on someone who didn't care for the social scene, and who didn't—in Coral's opinion—make the best of themselves.

Victoria stared at her mother, the little prickles running down her spine telling her she was about to hear something she didn't want to hear. But still she said, 'Go on,' her voice steady.

'Gina Rossellini—that second, or is it third cousin of Zac's?—took an overdose last night. She was in the room next to mine and there was such a commotion at about four o'clock this morning. *Stupid woman.*' The last two words were vicious. 'It's all for Zac's attention of course. I know her type.'

'Mother...' Victoria shook her head slowly, her sleek fall of silver-blonde hair that was cut in feathered wisps down to her shoulder blades shimmering under the artificial lights of the hotel lounge. 'What are you trying to tell me?' she asked quietly, her stomach doing a mighty cartwheel. 'Are you saying that there is something going on between Zac and Gina Rossellini?'

'She's been his mistress for years, girl; I thought you knew,' Coral said irritably. 'Everyone else on the planet does.'

'I... How could I know?' Victoria was suddenly aware of the moment in piercing detail—the subdued, discreet lighting overhead, the dusky pink carpet and luxurious furnishings, the faint perfume from the fresh flowers at the side of them—it was all stamped on her consciousness along with the horror of her mother's next words that chilled her blood to liquid ice.

'Well, it doesn't matter much one way or the other, does it?' Coral said matter-of-factly. 'Your father's mistress knew him long before I did and if you're wise you won't put anything in the way of *this* association continuing. A mistress is very useful, Victoria. She can take care of all that—' her mother flicked a languid hand with a distasteful wrinkle of her small nose '—side of things which men seem to find so important. As long as she knows her place—as Linda Ward did—she can be an asset to you.'

'Linda... Aunty Linda! You mean Aunty Linda was father's mistress?' Victoria asked faintly. She'd always known Linda Ward as one of her parents' close friends, although her mother had always treated the other woman with a patronising condescension Victoria hadn't understood until this very moment. 'And you didn't *mind*?'

'Of course not.' Her mother was clearly losing patience as she snapped, 'All men have mistresses, Victoria, if they can afford them. For heaven's sake open your eyes, girl. Of course one would prefer they have a little more control and discretion than Gina obviously has, but that comes of her having Latin blood, I suppose. Still, Zac's mother was Italian so I suppose Gina suits him in certain regards. Men look for different things in wives and mistresses,' Coral continued in the normal superior manner she adopted when talking to her daughter.

'Mistresses are for certain…basic needs; wives are chosen for their social connections and pedigree, and for the continuation of the family name if so required.'

'Zac…Zac isn't like that,' Victoria protested dazedly. 'I don't know what happened with Gina, but he isn't still seeing her, I know it. And he married me because he loves me, not because of my name or standing or anything like that,' she finished a trifle wildly, her hands clenching into two fists at her sides.

'Pull yourself together.' It was soft but deadly. 'Don't you dare cause a scene, Victoria. Of course Zac has a regard for you, but an alliance with the Chigley-Browns is also very useful to him. Your father's business interests were very far-reaching, and there is already a deal going through to cement an alliance.'

'I don't believe you.' Victoria glared at her. 'I don't.'

But her mother's sharp ears caught the soft quiver in the brave protest, and her hard blue eyes that resembled cold glass were piercing. Coral sighed irritably, before she snapped, 'I do hope you aren't going to be difficult about all this, Victoria. For a grown woman of twenty you really are most childish. Zac spent part of the night in Gina's room when he was called to her side—now face that and get on with things for goodness' sake. I don't know how many of our guests—' *ours*? thought Victoria numbly '—are aware of the situation, but you need to handle this with the sophistication Zac will naturally expect of his wife.'

'*I don't believe you.*' This time it was a fierce hiss, and Coral actually drew back in her chair, her light blue eyes wide with shock and surprise, as Victoria continued, 'You disgust me, do you know that? You have always disgusted me, although when I was younger I couldn't put a name to why. But you're shallow, utterly selfish, and you don't care about anyone but yourself. You've never loved me; I don't believe you've ever loved anyone.'

Victoria rose as she finished speaking, glaring down at her mother with blazing blue eyes. 'I'm going to find Zac now, and I know he'll tell me it was all lies. We want to have a real marriage, something you couldn't possibly understand.'

'*Victoria.*' Angry though her mother was, her voice still didn't rise above a certain level, her control absolute. 'Sit down at once and behave yourself. I'm ashamed of you.'

'I'm a married woman, Mother, and your time of telling me what to do is over,' Victoria said tightly. 'I couldn't believe the terrible scene you caused when I said I wanted to go to help the children in Romania, or the tactics you used to try and stop me going, but you failed then and you will continue to fail. I make my own decisions now; kindly remember that in future. And we will never agree on anything; I accept that now. We're worlds apart.'

She was shaking so much as she walked over to join Zac that he couldn't fail to notice, and as he finished his telephone call abruptly the thought did flash through Victoria's mind as to why he couldn't have used the phone in their suite.

'Tory?' It was his pet name for her and she welcomed the security of the intimacy for a moment. 'What's wrong?' He took her arm as he spoke, moving her into a quiet corner as he held her against his chest before moving her away slightly in order to look down into her face. 'Has someone upset you?'

'My...my mother.' Victoria breathed deeply, willing herself to remain strong. 'She said things, things about you and...Gina.'

'What things?' His voice was expressionless and calm, but Victoria had seen the impact in his eyes and her heart stopped before racing on like an express train. There *was* something in this.

'She said Gina was your mistress.' Victoria pulled away

from him now, standing straight and stiff as she looked intently into his face. 'And that your business interests are forming a merger with my father's. She said it's all been arranged for ages.'

'And?' He continued to look at her with the poker face she had seen him adopt with other people in other situations. But not her. Never with her. With her he had been open and warm and tender... Black foreboding took all the colour from her face.

'Isn't that enough?' Victoria asked tightly. 'Is it true?'

'Tory, let's go somewhere more private to discuss this.'

'Where did you go when you left our room last night?' she asked with painful dignity, holding her slender body ramrod-straight. 'Did you go to see Gina because she had taken an overdose?'

'Victoria, I'm not prepared to discuss this here.' The 'Tory' had gone, Victoria thought with grim discernment, and in that moment she knew whom he had been phoning too. Gina Rossellini.

'Why did she do that, Zac?' She ignored his furious frown with a regal composure her mother would have been proud of. 'Was it because she couldn't handle seeing you marry someone else? Because she'd thought *she* was going to be the one you took down the aisle, rather than becoming the one you kept on the side? And why did you marry *me* anyway? Were my connections better than hers? Have I swelled the Harding coffers?' she persisted stiffly.

'Is that what Coral told you?' he asked grimly.

But he hadn't denied it. *He hadn't denied it.* She couldn't believe this was happening to her. 'Zac, are you, or are you not, dealing with the people who now run my father's business interests for my mother with a view to an alliance?' Victoria asked woodenly. 'A simple yes or no will do.' She stared at him desperately.

'Yes.' And he didn't bat an eyelid. Not an eyelid.

'And did you spend part of the night with Gina when she called you after taking an overdose?' she continued flatly, her heart thudding as the nightmare escalated at his grim,

'Yes, I did.'

'And she is your mistress.'

It was a statement, not a question, and now his cool control was absolute when he said evenly, 'We had a relationship once, Victoria. Past tense.'

She wanted to believe him. She couldn't believe how much she wanted to—but she didn't. 'Why didn't you tell me about her before, Zac? Especially knowing she would be here at the wedding?' Victoria asked numbly. And she had actually *liked* Gina when she had met her, she thought with a stab of fierce self-disgust at her own credulity. She'd thought the other woman charming.

'She wasn't relevant to you and me,' he said softly. 'That's why.' He went to take her arm again but she jerked away tightly.

'Wasn't relevant?' What planet was this man on? What planet were they all on? Victoria asked herself bitterly. And then she remembered something Zac had let slip a couple of weeks before, and she felt her heart crack and break into a hundred tiny pieces.

'You had lunch with her recently,' she stated slowly, searching her memory. 'You said you were helping her buy an apartment, putting her in touch with the right people.' And now she stepped back a pace, her violet eyes black with pain. 'You were setting up a love nest, weren't you? And this morning, this morning—' She couldn't express how his withdrawal from her when she had first awoken was affecting her. *'I hate you,'* she said bitterly.

'Victoria!' He caught her arm as she went to swing away from him, forcing her to remain where she was. 'Listen to me, for crying out loud. *Listen.* I can explain all this.'

'You left me on our wedding night to go to her,' Victoria said slowly, her voice flat but her eyes expressing her shock and horror. 'You still care about her, don't you?

You still love her. *When she called you, you went to her and left me.'*

'Victoria, I married *you*,' he said with savage restraint, his fingers bruising the soft flesh of her arm. 'I love *you*.'

'Tell me you feel nothing for her. Tell me,' she insisted hotly. 'Tell me you didn't buy her that apartment, that I'm wrong.'

And then his eyes flickered again and she knew he wouldn't say it. Because he knew she would know he was lying.

'I'm going back to the room for a while; I want to be alone,' she said shakily. 'I'll join you and the others later.'

'I'm coming with you; this has gone far enough—'

'No.' She interrupted his angry voice with a sharp lift of her chin and a straightening of her body. 'I need...I need some time before I come into breakfast, and then...we can talk afterwards. I can't now; I just can't.' Her voice broke then, and as his face twisted and he would have taken her in his arms she backed away so sharply she almost fell over. She couldn't bear for him to touch her. She hated him. Oh, she hated him.

'Please, Zac,' she said with touching dignity, 'if you've ever had any feeling for me at all, let me have a few minutes by myself. I feel you owe me that at least.'

'This is crazy,' he ground out furiously through clenched teeth. 'Your damned mother wants shooting!'

'I'll see you in a few minutes.' Her voice was dismissive, and she didn't argue the point further, walking swiftly over to the lifts and entering the first one without turning her head. She had half expected him to follow, and by the time she reached their suite and realised he wasn't going to something had solidified in her heart, making it feel like a ten-ton weight.

Their bags were sitting in the corner, packed and labelled for their month's honeymoon in Jamaica, but Victoria took only her overnight case and handbag with her, leaving the hotel quietly by the back entrance through the kitchens to avoid Reception and the possibility that Zac might be there. Facing him again was unthinkable.

Once outside in the cool chill of the late March morning, she stood uncertainly looking from left to right along the side road bordering the rear of the hotel. She couldn't go to their beautiful new house in Wimbledon, or her mother's apartment in Kensington—they would be the first places Zac would look for her—and most of their friends' and relations' homes were out for the same reason. She bit her lip, her face desperate. And then it came to her. William. She could go to William.

William was the brother of one of her old schoolfriends, and she had known him since her first visit to her friend's house when she had been eight years old and terribly shy. He had teased her, played with her, and never once led her to believe he considered an eight-year-old girl beneath his fifteen-year-old notice.

For the next few years Victoria had spent most of the holidays from boarding-school with his family. Her mother had been only too pleased to be spared the inconvenience of having her around—something Coral had made abundantly clear several times—and when Victoria was thirteen, and the family had moved abroad, William had stayed in England. He had a very modern bachelor pad with enough gadgets for a James Bond movie, and she had still continued to visit him now and again before she had left England for the year in Romania.

He had a high-pressured and absorbing job in the BBC, which meant he was out of the country for weeks at a time on some assignment or other, but she knew he had been due home from the latest mission the night before. He had sent a polite note to her a couple of weeks ago to say he regretted he was going to miss the wedding by hours. So, more likely than not he would be in, and, best of all, Zac had never met him. In fact she wasn't even sure if Zac knew of the other man's existence.

William had been in—very in as it happened—and once

he had got dressed and the lady had left, insisting she had been due to leave in the next hour anyway, he had let Victoria cry herself into a frenzy and then out of it again. He had held her close, murmuring soothing nothings and asking no questions until she was calmer, at which point he had made a pot of very strong coffee and they had talked the afternoon away.

At the end of that time he'd offered her unconditional sanctuary for as long as she felt she needed it, with an additional invitation of the use of his holiday home in Tunisia which he'd recently inherited from his grandmother.

And she hadn't seen Zac again.

CHAPTER TWO

THERE was a wonderful aroma drifting through from the kitchen, and as Victoria came out of the tangle of her thoughts she found she was sniffing the air like a child. He really could cook.

'You look about twelve this morning.'

The deep, velvety soft voice from the doorway brought her head swinging round to see Zac watching her, his eyes very intent. She stared at him for a moment, and then shrugged carefully, her voice reserved as she said, 'Looks can be deceptive.' And in this case particularly so, she added silently. She was a grown woman with a child—his child—growing inside her. A bolt of something she recognised as fear shot through her, and she turned her head abruptly, hiding her face with the shining, silken veil of her hair. That piercing gaze was too perceptive by half, and it was one of Zac's strengths that he used mercilessly.

Zac mustn't know about the baby. Her mind was screaming a warning to her. In the dark days since their wedding she had come to realise she knew very little about the powerful, enigmatic man she had married so trustingly, but one thing she *did* know. He was the type of male who would fight tooth and nail for what was his, and he would certainly see this tiny being as belonging absolutely to the Harding empire. Her feelings would be incidental.

She had been raised in the care of nannies and chauffeurs and hired help and it had been miserable. She didn't intend to let that happen to her child. And it was hers, all hers, she told herself fiercely. It was even her mistake that meant it had been conceived at all. She had decided to take the pill several months before, but in all the furore

28

of the wedding she had forgotten that one, vital night, and a possible pregnancy had been the last thing on her mind when she had fled the next morning. She had just wanted to put as many miles between them as she could.

'Come and eat.' His voice was cool now, cool and hard, but she welcomed that. It emphasised that he was a stranger, that the man she had fallen in love with, the powerful, tender lover and fascinating companion, had been a figment of her wishful imagination, nothing more. *Her* Zac had never existed.

They ate at the tiny marbled breakfast bar that was just big enough to accommodate two plates, and Victoria had to admit that the light fluffy omelette and grilled fish doused in lemon and herbs were delicious. Zac had opened a bottle of wine he had found in the fridge, looking slightly surprised when Victoria insisted she only wanted a glass of orange juice but saying nothing.

But once the meal was finished and they had taken their coffee through to the sitting room he said plenty.

'Well?' Victoria had sat down in the rocking chair again but Zac remained standing, darkly brooding and slightly menacing as he leant against the far wall. 'Have you punished me enough or do you intend to continue with this charade?' he asked coolly.

'Charade?' It was only the thought of the damage black coffee would do to William's tasteful furnishings that saved him. 'You think this is a charade, a game, Zac? Think again,' Victoria said tightly as she placed the mug on the table next to her before temptation overcame her. How dared he stand there and say that?

But he had seen her hand tremble, and now he said, his voice grating, 'If you act like a child you should expect me to treat you like one. How could you leave like that, without saying a word? It was the height of stupidity.'

'But I am stupid, Zac.' Victoria glared at him, her pale skin stained scarlet and her jaw setting. 'I believed every

word you told me, didn't I? You can't get much more
stupid than that.'

'I have never lied to you,' he stated with outrageous
righteousness. And then, when she stared at him in furious
disbelief, her mouth opening and shutting as she sought
for a suitably cutting reply, he added, 'I can see that you
disagree with that.'

'You...you said you loved me,' she managed at last.

'I do love you, Victoria.' It was as cold as ice. 'It was
you who left *me*, remember? I didn't go anywhere.'

'And you think that unreasonable?' she asked incredulously. 'You leave me on our wedding night to go to
someone else—'

'I did not choose to leave you,' he said calmly, as
though that made everything all right. 'I answered a distress call from a human being who needed help, because
I was the only person who could.'

Of course you were, she thought with agonising pain—
you were the cause of it in the first place. 'You kept it a
secret,' she accused sharply. 'You didn't tell me what had
happened although you had several opportunities. You
weren't going to tell me, were you?'

'No, I was not.' It was not the answer Victoria had
expected; she had expected him to lie and perversely it
hurt all the more that he hadn't bothered to do even that.
'There was no need for you to be bothered with such
unpleasantness,' Zac said coolly. 'This was my problem,
and as such I dealt with it as I saw fit.'

Oh, it was his problem all right! 'You married me because you wanted to extend your business empire,'
Victoria stated with painful flatness, 'and don't bother to
deny it; I know it's true. You probably fancied me too,
and I was malleable enough—*stupid* enough—for your
purposes. You had planned to go on exactly as you'd always done, hadn't you? I wouldn't even have made a dent
in your life. There was to be no sharing, no real commitment.'

'That is all absolute rubbish and you know it,' he said angrily. 'I never lied to you, not once. If you had asked me about Gina, or the business deal with your mother's attorneys, I would have told you as much as you wanted to know.'

'That's easy to say now,' she shot back furiously, 'but how could I ask about something I didn't know a thing about?' She had always considered herself a quiet, gentle, easy-going sort of person, certainly not someone who would ever contemplate doing another human being serious physical harm, but right at that moment, if she had had anything in her hands, she would have thrown it straight at Zac's handsome, superior face. She wanted to hurt him. She wanted to really, *really* hurt him, and the knowledge shocked her more than she could express, acting like a bucket of cold water on the fire of her temper.

'Did you buy that apartment for Gina?' she asked now, her voice shaking. 'Just a few weeks before we got married? Did you?'

'I'm not answering that before I explain the circumstances,' he said after a long moment of looking at her white face from which all colour had fled.

'I think you just did,' she whispered numbly, her eyes desolate.

'Victoria, I had responsibilities I couldn't walk away from,' he bit back tightly. 'Responsibilities that necessitated action.'

'I know. Responsibilities to your mistress,' she said dully.

'No, to a member of my family,' he growled deeply. 'She is a distant cousin of mine, and her mother had phoned me from Italy to say that Gina had problems and needed help. I couldn't refuse her.'

'Did her mother know you were sleeping with her daughter?' Victoria asked with uncharacteristic cynicism.

'My affair with Gina ended before I met you,' Zac said

with rigid self-control. 'And that is the truth, Victoria. I swear it.'

'I don't believe you.' She stared at him with pain-filled eyes.

The words hung in the air for an eternity, and as Victoria wrenched her eyes from his and turned to stare out into the garden—anything to avoid looking at his face and seeing the look that had come into the dark eyes at her words—she focused on a small, flat, large-eyed lizard that had changed its colour to suit the large stone on which it was hanging by the tiny suckers on its toes.

How could life go on—the sun shine so brightly, the flowers and trees look so beautiful—when her world was ending? she asked herself silently. But she had to finish this now—it was even more important after what she had learnt that morning.

She had thought he was different, she'd believed he really loved her as she did him—and she *had* loved him, so much—but he was part of her mother's world, not hers. She didn't want to spend the rest of her life with a man whose values resembled those of her father. Her mother might have been able to handle it—in fact her mother had clearly relished it—but Victoria knew herself well enough to recognise she would destroy herself if she tried to do the same. The last two months had confirmed that if nothing else. But there was more, much more, she understood now.

And it wasn't just Gina, or even the merger, big as those issues were. In all their months of being together, in all the magic and laughter and joy, he had never really *talked* to her, she thought numbly. She had been like a pretty little doll to him, an entertaining novelty he had picked up and decided to buy, and she had been too captivated and under his spell to see the warning signs. But they had been there. And now she was taking notice.

She wanted her child brought up in the real world, with real people. It wouldn't be easy, but she wouldn't ask Zac or her mother for a penny. She would work—she would get a job doing anything, and she would make it by herself. She wanted nothing more to do with their seedy little world. It was over.

'Don't do this, Victoria.' Zac's voice was as cold as ice. 'You're throwing away something precious because of hurt pride, that's all. Let me explain; let's talk it through from the beginning.' And then, more urgently, he said, 'It'll be all right, *trust me.*'

'It's too late.' She turned back to him then, her blue eyes with their long thick lashes shadowed with pain. 'It's all far, far too late. We should never have married, Zac. We're worlds apart in everything that matters. And you know it too, deep down.'

'The hell we are,' he ground out in savage denial. '*The hell we are.* You're my wife and I don't let go of what is mine.'

He reached her in three angry strides, pulling her up out of the rocking chair and into his arms with a fury that was all the more intense for being suppressed, his mouth fastening on hers.

She was too stunned at first to fight him, and then, as she began to twist and turn in his hold, the smell and taste and feel of him began to spin in her head. She had been starving for this, physically starving for long, wretched, tear-filled weeks, and as he devoured her mouth desire rose hot and strong in her veins. But it would be madness to give in to it.

She still continued to struggle, the knowledge of her weakness where this man was concerned shameful and humiliating, but she was fighting herself more than him and she knew it. She was aware of the power in his muscled body, and also that he was using his strength to restrain rather than force her, but his mouth was hungry and urgent and inciting a response in the depth of her she didn't want to give. *Dared* not give.

'Don't…don't do this.' Her voice was shaking and frantic.

'Why not?' He raised his head slightly, his eyes glittering and black as he moved her back against the whitewashed wall of the sitting room. 'I've been thinking of nothing else for weeks.'

'I don't want to,' she protested tremblingly, moving her head as he tried to take her lips again. 'And I don't want you—*I don't*.'

'Yes, you do,' he growled thickly. He was breathing raggedly, his body taut and his thighs hard against hers. 'That night, our wedding night, was just a taste for both of us. I want more, much more. You're mine, Tory; you'll always be mine…'

She froze, the blood turning to liquid ice in her veins. Was this what the great love she had thought they'd shared had been reduced to? An animal mating, the satisfaction of physical lust, the possessor taking the possession he had acquired? He didn't love her—he didn't know what love was. None of his kind did. Her mind continued to race as he began to kiss her again.

He had bought an apartment for Gina just weeks before they had got married. He had gone to her, on their wedding night, the minute Gina had called. And there had been a big incentive for him to rush *her* down the aisle— a lucrative deal for all concerned.

He had taken her as his wife because she met all the criteria he had laid down for the future Mrs Harding, and because, as he had said more than once during their engagement, it was time he settled down and became a family man. He wanted children, and she was a suitable breeding machine. But he hadn't been prepared to cut the tie with Gina in the last resort. And she *hated* him.

He couldn't fail to notice her rigidity, and after a moment he swore under his breath, raising his head as he said, 'Don't fight me, Tory. You're mine and you know it. You can't win.'

Maybe not, but I can make sure you don't win either, she thought numbly. 'I want a divorce, Zac.' As he moved back a pace, his eyes narrowing on her face, she raised her chin determinedly. 'As soon as possible,' she added, with such a note of determination in her voice he couldn't fail to believe she meant business.

'No way.' It was almost lazy, only the fiery glow in his black eyes revealing the banked-down emotion. 'No way.'

'I mean it,' she insisted with quiet dignity.

'So do I.' The desire which still had him in its grip was making his voice husky. 'I told you, I never let go of what is mine. Not unless I want to, that is. And in this case I don't.'

She almost put her hand protectively across her flat stomach as he spoke, before warning herself she couldn't afford any instinctive gestures like that. Zac was nobody's fool. She had to get back to England and then disappear again, until the divorce was through or the baby was born—whichever came first. And the fewer people who knew about the pregnancy the better.

'You won't be able to stop me divorcing you, Zac,' Victoria said with a quiet bravery she hadn't known she was capable of. 'It will happen whether you want it to or not. No woman has to remain chained to a man she doesn't love these days.'

'Ah, but you do love me.' It was supremely arrogant and devastatingly true, and Victoria kept her face blank only by the harsh training she had received throughout a childhood of hiding her feelings. Then, as now, she had known any weakness would be recognised and used unmercifully against her. 'I was the first man to take you and I intend to be the last. Believe me.'

She couldn't *believe* the double standards. 'I take it you operate on the sentiment that a woman is like a flower with honey for just one bee?' she said bitterly. 'Whereas a man is able to go from flower to flower to flower? Is that it?'

'I didn't say that.' He eyed her darkly, his mouth grim.

'You didn't have to,' she returned smartly. 'That particular male view has been expressed since the beginning of time; it's not new. Men can play around all they like but the little woman remains at home as pure as the driven snow.'

'I never pretended that I was inexperienced, Victoria,' Zac ground out irritably. 'You knew when you married me that there had been other women before you. I was quite open about that.'

'*Before* me, yes.' She drew in a shuddering breath, the now familiar feeling of light-headedness and nausea rearing its head. 'I just didn't expect there would be any after me, that's all. Look—' she sank down into the rocking chair again, her head bowed as she tried to control the nausea '—we're getting nowhere with all this and I'm not feeling too well; the heat and the different food has upset my stomach. Please go, Zac. I need to lie down.'

Her extreme pallor spoke for itself, and after an exasperated, 'For crying out loud,' Zac took a visible hold on his temper before saying, his voice quieter, 'All right, I'll leave you to rest. But Victoria?' She raised her head at the tone, looking at him for a long moment as he surveyed her with narrowed eyes before saying, 'Don't think about disappearing again. Once I can accept, but twice would be a big, big mistake. Do I make myself clear?' he added grimly.

Who did he think he was talking to—one of his employees? Victoria thought furiously, the adrenalin pumping hot and strong. She raised her drooping head a few notches and glared at him.

The anger carried her through the next few moments of Zac leaving, but it left her in a big whoosh when he turned on the doorstep, putting down his big black leather overnight bag that he had obviously slung into her hall some time during his arrival, and took her in his arms again, kissing her very thoroughly before raising dark, sardonic eyebrows at her flushed protestations.

'I can't help it,' he said mockingly. 'There's something about this pale and interesting look that turns me on, especially with the new fiery part of you as an interesting contrast.'

'I don't want you to be turned on.' She wasn't at all sure it was the truth and that confused her still more. 'Not now, not ever.'

'Thanks a bunch.' It was very dry.

'I mean everything I've said today, Zac—'

'No, you don't,' he interposed smoothly, before she could say anything more. 'You want me every bit as much as I want you, but you don't trust me and I don't like that. I don't like that at all.'

'You don't like it?' She stared at him incredulously, unable to believe her ears. 'Well, that's just tough, isn't it?'

He shrugged lazily, but Victoria had seen his eyes narrow and his mouth tighten. She hadn't spoken to him like that before and he didn't like it. Good. The man's arrogance was past belief and she wasn't prepared to take it a minute longer.

'You're really not going to listen to me, are you?' he said thoughtfully after a tense few seconds had ticked by. 'But you believed every word the dragon lady said.'

His nickname for her mother used to make Victoria smile but she didn't feel like smiling any more. And now, in spite of the muggy, sweltering heat that had the dusty streets deserted and empty except for a few chickens pecking desultorily here and there, the temperature chilled to zero as he added, 'And you ran to William Howard; you *trust* William Howard. Why is that, Victoria?'

'William?' In the shock of seeing Zac again she hadn't thought to ask exactly how he had known where she was, but now her voice trembled as she said, 'Did William tell you where I was? You...you haven't hurt him—'

Now it was arctic conditions. 'No, I haven't hurt him,' Zac grated with dangerous composure, his eyes lethal. 'I wasn't aware that there was any reason to, but I'm beginning to wonder. I found out where you were by other means; I have...contacts.'

Oh, yes, she was well aware of his 'contacts', Victoria thought bitterly. He had a small army of minions ready to jump at the click of his fingers, and money could buy anything—or anyone. She had heard him talk about 'necessary research' once—they had been at a party and one of his business colleagues had button-holed him about a prospective deal—and when she had asked him what he had meant, once the man was gone, he had smiled before saying, 'I have people who find out things, Tory, that's all. Things that other people might prefer to keep hidden.'

'Private detectives, you mean?' she had asked naively.

'Something like that.' And then he had changed the subject.

'Why doesn't Coral know this William?' Zac asked sharply.

Victoria snapped back from the past as Zac's voice cut into her thoughts. 'My mother never took any interest in my friends,' Victoria said tightly, 'as well you know.' Except you, she thought. My mother took a great interest in you from day one. And now she knew why. 'Have you asked her about William?' she added abruptly as the portent of his words made itself known. Silly question; of course he had.

'Yes, I have.' The night-black eyes were boring into her brain. 'He is the brother of a schoolfriend, yes? That is all that Coral knew. My...source informed me he was out of the country covering some disturbance or other in Saudi Arabia.'

'That's top-secret information,' Victoria blurted out, shocked to the core. William had impressed upon her, on his last visit the previous weekend, that only very few people knew of his forthcoming, extremely sensitive and delicate assignment.

'But he told you,' Zac said very softly. 'He told you, Victoria.'

'Of course he did.' She had meant that William had confided his whereabouts to her because she was an old and trusted friend who was living in his home—or one of them—and Victoria knew William had been trying to prevent her worrying if she was unable to contact him for a week or two. But now, as she stared into the menacingly dark face of her husband, she realised Zac had put quite another interpretation on her innocent reply.

'Of course.' His mouth was a hard, angry line, his black brows drawn together in a ferocious scowl. 'Victoria, exactly what *is* your relationship with this action man?' Zac asked with icy control. 'And I want the truth, please,' he added cuttingly.

'My...' He was jealous. He was jealous of *William*, Victoria thought numbly. And who was *he* to talk about truth?

'You flew out to Tunisia in the middle of April,' Zac bit out harshly, looking every inch his mother's son as his glittering black eyes blazed his Italian blood. 'Where were you for the two weeks before that when you fell off the face of the earth?'

He was questioning *her* morals? Victoria thought disbelievingly, white-hot rage beginning to bubble like a volcano about to explode. He was actually *daring* to suggest that she and William...

'*How dare you?*' she spluttered helplessly, utterly outraged.

'Oh, I dare, Victoria. I most certainly dare,' he snarled darkly, breaking into her loud, hissing protest with a fury that matched her own. 'I'm asking you again—where were you?'

She glared at him, drawing herself up to her full five feet six inches as she tilted back her head and stared him straight in the eyes. 'I was at William's flat,' she said icily. 'Okay?'

'I see.' It was more ominous than any bellow.

'No, you don't! You don't see at all,' Victoria shot back tightly. 'William has been absolutely wonderful to me, he always has been, but we're friends, that's all. Platonic friends.'

'There is no such thing between a man and woman,' Zac stated tautly, 'especially a woman who looks like you. He would have to be made of stone, and I take it he is very much a flesh-and-blood man, right? A man who likes women?' He added suddenly, evidence that he had thought of another possibility clear on his face.

'Of course William likes women.' Victoria was even more furious that Zac obviously considered the only way she and William had been able to keep their hands off each other was if William preferred men. 'He's very...' Her voice stopped abruptly as she realised it wasn't tactful in the circumstances to labour William's masculinity. She stared at him as her mind went blank.

'Very...?' Zac rasped angrily. 'William is very...?'

Oh, to hell with it. 'Male,' Victoria said a trifle weakly.

'Is he?' If ever two words were loaded, those two were. 'And this very male man looks on you in the same way an aged uncle would?' Zac continued with heavy sarcasm. 'How old is he?'

'Twenty-seven.' Victoria's tone clearly stated, Make of that what you will. 'And I'm not prepared to discuss William with you,' she added firmly, contradicting herself immediately when she said, 'He, at least, has never let me down.'

'I bet he hasn't,' Zac derided contemptuously, 'but if you ever stay with him again you'd better book him a hospital bed at the same time. He'll need one.' He glared at her ferociously.

'You wouldn't!' Victoria glared back, horrified. 'How

dare you threaten William? He's never done anything to you.'

'It's not what he's done to *me* that concerns me,' Zac said with lethal intent. 'And it's not a threat, it's a promise.'

'I don't believe this!' She was so angry she could barely get the words out. 'After all you've done, you have the cheek to object to William and me—' She suddenly had a wave of light-headedness and stopped abruptly, her colour coming and going as she stared into the blazingly angry face of her husband.

'William and you…?' Zac pressed softly, his face making it clear he was thinking the worst from her sudden silence.

'Being friends.' Even to her own ears it sounded like an afterthought, and her own patheticness made her voice tremble with a mixture of rage and injured pride as she said, 'It is your suspicious mind that has made up the rest. William is one of the nicest men I know, and certainly the most honourable. He's kind and generous—'

'Spare me a list of his virtues, Victoria, please,' Zac grated with hateful sarcasm. 'I'm amazed this paragon hasn't got wings already. And whilst we're talking about suspicious minds, might I remind you you are in no position to cast the first stone?'

'You're saying I've got a suspicious mind?' Her voice had risen to a shrill shriek that made Zac wince. 'After you—' She couldn't go on, she was too angry, and it was a few gasping breaths later before she managed to say, 'I'm not discussing this any more, there's absolutely no point, but I can't believe you just said that.'

'One rule for you and one rule for me?' Zac suggested icily. It was adding salt to the wound.

'I'm going to lie down.' Victoria drew herself up, her voice fairly coherent, which was a miracle in itself considering how she was feeling. 'I'm…I'm feeling worse.' Worse? She felt ghastly.

'Whereas I, of course, am feeling great?' came the sarcastic rejoinder. And then, when she didn't venture a comment, he asked, 'Do you want the number of my hotel?'

'No.'

Victoria shut the door on his outraged face and just made it to the bathroom before she deposited the contents of her stomach into William's bright blue basin.

CHAPTER THREE

'AND you haven't told him you're pregnant?'

It was a full week later and Victoria was back in England, the crowded restaurant where she and William were having lunch packed to bursting with the élite of London's high-fliers.

'No, I told you. He was only in Tunisia overnight, and when he came back in the evening we just fought again. It...it was awful.' Victoria wanted to cry but she knew she couldn't—not in the middle of Radstone's where her lettuce leaves and chicken must be costing William a small fortune. 'I told him I was coming back to England and...and that I'd be renting a place.' She hadn't told William the full story—William, like Zac, had a healthy amount of fierce male pride, and she doubted he would appreciate being labelled the third part of a triangle.

It seemed she was less adept at hiding the truth than she had thought. 'I take it he objected to you staying at Mimosa?' William asked wryly with a lift of his dark eyebrows. 'And even more my flat, no doubt. Well, I can understand that of course.'

'But *why*?' Victoria objected plaintively. 'I told him we were old friends, and that our relationship was purely platonic, but he didn't believe me. He...said that there was no such thing as a platonic friendship between a man and a woman.'

'He was right,' William agreed with a remarkable lack of heat.

It wasn't what Victoria had expected, and her face said so.

'Look, Blue-eyes—' it was the nickname he had given

her when she was eight years old and had stuck ever since '—you're absolutely gorgeous, and I fancy you like mad, but I've always known you see me as a big brother and nothing more. So...' He shrugged easily, his nonchalance hiding a pain which had plagued him for years and had taken more self-will than he had known he possessed to come to terms with. 'That's okay. I'd rather be in your life as a friend than out of it altogether.' He shrugged slowly.

'Oh, William.' She stared at him, her soft heart immediately flooded with guilt. 'You've never said... I didn't *know*.'

'Of course you didn't, and it's no big deal,' he insisted easily. No big deal? She still had the power to floor him with one look from those big blue eyes. 'I'm here for you, always, okay? And all the crazy, angry husbands in the world wouldn't make me change my mind. My home is your home, Blue-eyes, whenever you need it. No strings, no bother. Now—' he smiled at her as the moment became charged with emotion '—eat your lunch. You're eating for two, remember, so you'd better pack away a double dessert to make up for the lack of nutrition in that thing.' He poked his fork at her salad with manly distaste.

'William...' Victoria wriggled helplessly, her eyes tragic.

'Eat, woman.' And this time his smile was genuine. 'It's not the end of the world. I'm not going to die from unrequited love or anything like that. You know me—tough as old boots.'

'I feel awful,' Victoria murmured softly.

'Well, don't.' And suddenly it was the old William, the William she knew—or thought she had known, she corrected silently. 'I'm not exactly short of female company as you well know.' He gave a leery wink to make her laugh, and Victoria obliged, although it was forced. Poor William. Poor, *poor* William.

She just hadn't dreamt William felt like that about her,

she told herself in amazement. Not in a hundred years. In fact she was beginning to think that the whole male population was a species apart. Why hadn't he *said* something? She glanced at him now as he tucked into an enormous fillet steak with every appearance of enjoyment, to all intents and purposes perfectly relaxed.

Could she have ever felt that certain spark with William? He was certainly good-looking, with his wavy dark hair and brown eyes with little flecks of green, straight nose and smiling mouth. He was tall too, not as tall as Zac's six feet four, but William was a good six inches taller than her and lean and fit with it. But he was right. She lowered her eyes to her plate and pecked at her salad. She *did* look on him as a brother. Loved him as a brother actually... But there was nothing romantic there.

'How long does this morning sickness go on?' William asked suddenly, and she glanced up to see a look of concern in his gentle eyes. 'You're getting as thin as a rake.'

'A few more weeks yet, I think.' She sighed wearily. 'And I only wish it *was* morning sickness. With me it's every hour of the day and night sickness, and then a bit. I was even sick in the middle of the night when I got up to go to the loo. And that's another inconvenient something no one tells you about—my bladder has developed a life of its own,' she finished plaintively.

'Poor old love.' But he was laughing and she couldn't help a rueful grin back, which swiftly faded when he said, his tone serious now, 'You do know you're going to have to tell him sooner or later? It's his child too, Blue-eyes. You can't keep something like that from a man. This idea of disappearing is a non-starter.'

'What's this, the eternal brotherhood?' she asked grumpily. But he was right. She knew he was right. And she also knew she was going to have the dickens of a fight on her hands once Zac knew she was carrying his child. But she wasn't going to give in.

They left the restaurant arm in arm, and as always

Victoria felt better for having talked to William, after crying most of the long, lonely night away, lying awake until the early hours.

She had moved into the tiny, one-bedroomed flat she was renting the day before, and amazingly it had been her mother who had been instrumental in her finding the little treasure of a place tucked away in Richmond. It belonged to the daughter of one of Coral's bridge partners, apparently, who was away working in America for twelve months and had decided to rent out if she could get a suitable lodger. Victoria was considered suitable, and so that was that and she was installed before she knew it.

Victoria had been only too grateful to find somewhere so quickly—the three days she had spent at her mother's apartment on her return to England had been more than enough for both women. And how Coral would react when she found out she was going to be a grandmother, Victoria didn't even like to contemplate. She was barely speaking to her daughter as it was, and Coral had told her flatly—in the first minute of their meeting on Victoria's return to England—that she considered Victoria totally responsible for the breakdown of her marriage.

As though he had picked up her thoughts, William stopped her on the pavement just outside the restaurant and enclosed her lightly in his arms, looking down into her face as he said, 'How is your mother behaving in all this, or don't I need to ask?'

'About as you'd expect,' Victoria said with justified bitterness. 'Everything is all my fault and Zac can't do anything wrong.'

'She's one on her own. It's hard to believe—'

Victoria never did find out what William found hard to believe, because in the next moment, as she stood relaxed in his arms, her head tilted as she looked up into the face of this tried and trusted friend, a dark, cold voice at the side of them brought her jerking out of William's hold as though something had bitten her. Which in a way it had, she thought shakily as her heart continued to beat like a crazy thing.

'I hate to interrupt what is obviously a tender moment, but I want a word with my wife.' Ice tinkled in every word.

'Zac.' Victoria stumbled backwards and would have fallen but for Zac's quick hand at her elbow, which immediately returned to his side when she was steady, as though he couldn't bear to touch her. 'What...? How did you...?' she stammered incoherently.

'Let's cut the "what are you doing here?" scenario,' Zac grated with icy contempt. 'I'm sure we can do better than that.'

He looked magnificent. That was Victoria's first jumbled thought. Followed by, And angry. Definitely furiously, *murderously* angry. He was in a business suit, clearly having come from the office, and in spite of the rage that was turning the dark eyes into brilliantly black bullets and his beautifully chiselled mouth into a hard, straight line his control was absolute.

'Zac, this isn't a good moment,' she began tremblingly.

'On the contrary, Victoria, it is an excellent moment,' he said tightly, his eyes sweeping over her flushed, anxious face.

'I'm... I've just had lunch. This is—'

'William Howard,' Zac finished for her, giving the other man one scathing glance before turning back to Victoria again. 'Now say goodbye to your playmate because we've got some serious talking to do, the results of which will determine whether lover boy here needs a new face in the very near future.'

'What on earth are you talking about?' She stared at him in horrified amazement. His voice hadn't been raised one iota above normal, which made the content of his words all the more incredible.

'It's very simple, Victoria, but not something to be discussed in the middle of the street,' Zac said with smooth control, only the lethal glitter in the black eyes betraying the rage he was hiding.

'Now just hang on a minute.' William had had enough of being ignored. 'Perhaps Victoria doesn't want to come with you.'

'Surprisingly I really don't care what Victoria wants,' Zac said with smooth venom, and then, as William went to say more, he added with biting savagery, 'Stay out of this, Howard.'

'Zac, have you gone mad?' Victoria asked faintly. 'Stop this.'

'One of us has, and don't try to tell me what to do.'

'She's not coming with you the mood you're in,' William said stoutly. 'Not without me as well, that is.'

'Wrong,' Zac rasped. 'Quite wrong.'

'You hurt her and I'll—' William knew immediately he had said the worst thing possible in the circumstances as Zac turned to him, with a lightning move of his formidable body, and but for Victoria moving even quicker between them William knew he wouldn't have been on his feet for many more seconds.

'Zac, *please…*' Victoria was hanging onto his arms now, but as Zac stared at the other man over her head William doubted if the enraged man in front of him even heard her.

'I wouldn't harm a hair of her head,' Zac grated out harshly, 'and she knows it. You, however, are a different matter.'

'Zac, you said you wanted to talk, so come on.' Victoria would have gone anywhere, said anything in that moment to get some safe distance between the two men. 'Where's your car?' She glanced wildly about the pavement as though she expected Zac's beautiful Jaguar to be sitting beside them like an obedient pet dog.

'Over there.' Zac gestured behind her without taking his glittering eyes off William for a moment, but although his voice was calmer Victoria could feel the bunched muscles under her fingers and she didn't dare let go of him.

'You don't have to go with him,' William said softly, looking straight into Victoria's terrified eyes now. 'His threats don't worry me in the least, Blue-eyes. You know that.'

The pet name had come naturally to his lips, but as Victoria felt Zac tense and heard him growl, 'They ought to, Howard, if you want to stay alive,' she knew it had enraged Zac further.

'I want to go, William. We...have things to talk about, you know?' Victoria said meaningfully. 'It might as well be now.'

William understood what she was saying and nodded slowly. 'Okay, whatever you say.' And then Victoria had to hold onto Zac all the more tightly as William looked at the other man and added, 'And the strong-arm tactics weren't necessary. If she hadn't chosen to go with you no power on earth would have made me let her go. I just wanted to make that perfectly clear, okay?'

'You young—'

Victoria hung on like grim death.

But William had gone, turning swiftly with one last nod at Victoria and disappearing into the lunchtime throng, who had ignored the little drama being enacted amongst them in the cold, disinterested way peculiar to all big cities.

'Did I detect a hidden meaning in that somewhat cryptic statement regarding our proposed chat?' Zac asked with lethal sarcasm as—William having vanished—he took Victoria's arm and led her over to his car. 'I take it I won't like it, right?'

'I...I don't know what you mean,' she prevaricated weakly, hearing her words with very real self-disgust. She had to tell him about the baby for goodness' sake, she told herself firmly; it wasn't exactly something that could remain hidden for long. She was almost fourteen weeks pregnant, and the fact that a tiny little person was alive inside her, growing, changing, developing, was thrilling her more and more with every day that passed, in spite of her marriage breakdown. She loved this baby. She hadn't seen it, she didn't know if it was a boy or a girl, but she loved it with all her heart. It was part of her and part of Zac, and *nothing* could take that away from her. Nothing…and no one.

'I mean— Oh, forget it,' Zac said curtly, glancing once at her pale face as he opened the passenger door for her to slide into the luxurious interior of the XJ220, and then, after closing the door, striding round to the driver's seat and joining her before he spoke again. 'In spite of this abandoned lifestyle you seem to have taken up with such enthusiasm, you don't look particularly happy,' he said tightly. 'What's the matter? Isn't the grass as green as you thought? Regretting your fling already?'

'My *what*?' she bit back furiously, her back straightening.

'What would you call it, then?' he asked grimly as he pulled out into the teeming traffic after checking his mirrors. 'An intrigue? An illicit amour meant to heap retribution on my wicked, sinful head? How far has it gone, Victoria? Have you slept with this…old friend? And don't tell me the poor guy isn't crazy about you because a blind man could see it,' he finished caustically.

There was one lightning glance at her face—now suffused with burning colour—and then he concentrated on the view out of the windscreen as he nodded slowly. 'I see.' It was very bitter and very cold. 'So that's how it is.'

What did he see? Victoria asked herself confusedly. She felt awful about William, painfully guilty that she had been unaware of his real feelings for her. She would never have run to him for help if she had known, or accepted his invitation to live in his home; it must have been so difficult for him to maintain the kind, brotherly attitude he had always shown her when she was actually *living* with him in his own house, but he'd never faltered once.

'So.' Zac cut up an inoffensive motorist with vicious disregard. 'What do you want to do, Victoria?'

'I...I need to talk to you about something.' She couldn't tell him he was going to be a father in one breath, and that she had no intention of ever coming back to him in the other, in the midst of all this crazy traffic—there'd be a multi-car pile-up if she did. 'Could we pull in somewhere quiet for a minute or two, please?' she asked tentatively, her stomach churning.

'Ah, now why do I think I'm going to hear what you were just discussing with good old William?' Zac asked tightly. 'I am, aren't I?' he added brusquely. 'And cut the pussy-footing.'

'Yes.' She took a long hard breath and prayed for calm. He was so angry, so bitter, so *furious*, and it should be she who felt like this. *She* was the wronged one, not him, and she was blowed if she was going to explain her relationship with William any further. She had tried to do that twice in Tunisia and on each occasion he had twisted everything she'd said until even she had begun to believe black was white. It was all impossible.

He had his mistress and his nice little business deal— fine. But she wasn't part of the package, and neither was her child.

They didn't speak again as the powerful sleek car wove in and out of the traffic, the summer sun beating down outside the air-conditioned vehicle with fierce intensity. Victoria was breathlessly aware of the big masculine body so close to hers, the familiar delicious smell of him, the dark bronzed good looks and devastating presence turning her insides to jelly. How was she going to get through the rest of her life without him? she asked herself desperately. Knowing he was in the world, living, breathing, talking, laughing, and that she no longer figured in his life? Would Gina last? Would he stay with her? Or would there be other women? But there would be the baby; that, at least, would make her special. And he *had* married her. She had been his wife—if only for a night. One night to last a lifetime.

But Gina would have him much longer. The thought came from nowhere and caused her excruciating pain, and it was all she could do not to moan out loud. She didn't want to love him, and in the first caustic days after their wedding she had told herself she hated him, but it was no good—he was part of her in a way that no other man ever could be. She resented his hold over her in view of his infidelity, and she would never let him know how much she loved him, but she would never get over him. Zac Harding was too tough an act to follow. She sat in silent misery, staring blindly through the window as the waves of bitter anguish and despair ebbed and flowed. Till death do you part…for her.

When Zac pulled the car off the road and through a pair of wide-open iron gates, Victoria didn't realise at first where she was, and then, as she came out of the dark abyss of her thoughts, she sat up straight in her seat, her voice high as she said, 'Where…? I don't want to come here.'

'You said you wanted somewhere quiet to talk,' Zac said with dangerous coolness. 'Where could be quieter or more discreet than our home? The home we chose together, the home I live in alone.'

'It's not *our* home.' She fairly spat the words at him, the agony that had gripped her at seeing the place where she had thought she was going to be so happy making her voice savage.

'Yes, it is, Victoria.' In stark contrast to her fevered protest his voice was silky soft, the thread of steel that underlined his words making them all the more distinct in their lack of expression. 'Yours and mine, like it or not.'

'No.' She hardly knew what she was saying, so great was her distress. 'I renounce all claim to it.'

'Victoria, this is not the Reformation and you are not

Martin Luther,' Zac said with mordant cynicism as he watched her face with cruel eyes. 'No one has to renounce anything.'

'Well, I do.' She had faced the fact that she was never going to live here as a married woman some weeks ago, but she could still picture each room in her mind's eye. They had had such fun choosing the carpets and curtains, the wonderful antique furniture and new fitted kitchen. It had been such a beautiful dream...

The Victorian white-washed house had had an abundance of wisteria draping gracefully over the walls in May, but now, at the beginning of July, a cascading ramble of velvet-petalled roses were wafting their delicious perfume into the car as Zac opened his door, the tranquillity at odds with the tumult in her soul.

Victoria had fallen in love with the small but exquisite front garden before she had even set foot inside the house some months ago when she and Zac were searching out a property. It was full of flowers nestling in informal beds, but the snowdrops and crocuses of spring had given way to peonies, crimson poppies and fragrant roses of all colours that blazed out a riotous welcome now.

On entering the house in January, Victoria had found the large oak-dominated hall, with its winding staircase and mellow wooden floor, enticingly reminiscent of another, more tranquil era. It was a house in which to raise a family, she had told Zac excitedly on their first viewing, the sunlight streaming in through the sash windows and the big high-ceilinged rooms that reflected every scrap of light and space, her idea of a real home.

Zac had smiled indulgently at her enthusiasm, whilst pointing out the pitfalls of an older house, but he had bought it the next day, warts and all. And now she would never live in it.

'I don't want to go inside,' Victoria insisted again as Zac opened the passenger door and held out his hand to help her alight. 'We can talk just as well in the car, can't we?'

'Don't be ridiculous.' He had never spoken to her with such scathing disdain, but she preferred his ridicule to stepping inside the home she had dreamt about more times than she would like to remember over the last few weeks. And the dreams always had one conclusion—she and Zac entwined in their enormous king-size bed, the wildly expensive silk sheets which Zac had insisted on with wicked relish soft and sensuous beneath her naked limbs. 'What do you think I'm going to do—take you by force as soon as the front door closes?' he asked derisively. 'Now come and have a coffee and let's at least pretend to be two civilised people.'

She didn't feel civilised, Victoria thought miserably as she scrambled reluctantly out of the car, ignoring his outstretched hand and nearly sprawling headlong into the drive as a result of her defiance. In fact every time she thought of him with Gina she wanted to bite and kick and destroy. She just hoped the article she had read a day or so ago in one of the mother magazines she had bought, which stated that the unborn child picked up its mother's thoughts and brain patterns, was wrong. Otherwise she'd be giving birth to a miniature Rambo with psychopathic tendencies.

The hall was as beautiful as she remembered it, the two Shaker-style wooden chairs with floral-style woven silk seats at either side of an antique chest on which a vase crammed full of trailing roses stood looking just as she had pictured they would. They had been due to be delivered the first week of their honeymoon, and so Victoria hadn't seen them in residence before.

She felt the tears begin to well up and spoke quickly, her voice clipped, to quell the flow. 'The chairs look very nice.'

'Damn the chairs.' It was pure Zac, and in any other circumstances would have brought forth a smile. Now laughter was the last thing on her mind as Victoria followed the big, broad figure of her husband through to the huge farmhouse kitchen at the back of the house, which opened up on to a large and very gracious Victorian conservatory. 'Sit down.' Zac indicated one of the plumply upholstered cane sofas dotted about the conservatory through the open kitchen doors. 'I'll bring the coffee through.'

The back garden was a good deal larger than the front, about a third of an acre in all, and laid mainly to lawn with a thick border of mature trees and bushes that shielded the grounds from being overlooked. A few apple and pear trees dotted the lawned area, along with strategically placed benches positioned to benefit their occupants of the leafy shade, and it was to one of these that Victoria made her way, walking right through the conservatory and out into the sleeping garden.

The air was thick with the scents of summer, the air slumberous and still in the July heat, and as Victoria sank down onto the warm wood she found her legs were trembling and weak with trepidation.

She had to tell him about the baby *now*—she should have done it that day a week ago, Victoria thought miserably, leaning her head back against the smooth wood and shutting her eyes. That was another thing she didn't understand, this overwhelming tiredness she felt all the time. Even on the nights she did sleep well she woke up just as exhausted, and she *hated* feeling like this. She hated feeling tearful, she hated the constant nausea, she just hated everything, although it was some small comfort to know from the other pregnant women at the clinic that a good few of them felt just the same.

Self-pity threatened to overwhelm her, and she pushed it away determinedly, settling herself more comfortably on the sun-warmed bench. A lone aeroplane droned monotonously in the cloudless blue sky above, and Victoria could hear the odd bee or two buzzing for pollen in the background, but suddenly it was too much effort to open her eyes.

When Zac joined her she would tell him about the baby whilst emphasising she still wanted a divorce, and then the peace would be well and truly shattered, she thought wearily. For now she was taking a minute or two to rest in the calm before the storm; she had a feeling she was going to need it.

When Victoria next opened her eyes it was with the sensation that she was struggling up through layers of thick cotton wool, the exhaustion that had blanketed her senses taking a second or so to fade as she tried to adjust her mind to where she was.

The air was cooler. That was the first thing that registered in her dazed mind. And the dusky shadows of evening were beginning to stretch across the lawn. That was the second. The third was Zac's intent, narrowed gaze as she turned her head and saw him stretched out on a blanket at the side of her, an open briefcase and scattered papers all around him telling her he had been working while she had slept. And working for some time by all accounts.

'Oh, I'm sorry.' Victoria couldn't believe she had fallen asleep like that, her horrified face speaking for itself as she struggled upright, and hot colour staining her cheeks scarlet. 'What time is it?' she asked confusedly. 'Is it late?'

'Just gone seven,' Zac said expressionlessly.

'Seven?' She had slept for over five hours, she thought feverishly. What must he be thinking?

She found out what he was thinking when Zac said, his voice still level and even, 'Victoria, I'm going to ask you something, and I want a truthful answer. Are you ill?'

'What? No, no, I'm not ill,' she said hastily. She hadn't wanted it to be as abrupt as this, but suddenly there was no other way to say it. 'I'm…I'm expecting a baby. That's what I wanted to talk to you about,' she said hesitantly, feeling suddenly shy.

He didn't move a muscle, not even a flicker of those thick black eyelashes, and Victoria found herself beginning to babble as she continued, 'That's…that's why I'm not feeling too good at the moment—morning sickness and all that. Of course it's natural, perfectly natural, but that doesn't help much when it's happening.' She stopped abruptly; she was handling this all wrong. 'I'm sorry I didn't tell you before, in Tunisia,' she said more slowly, 'but I just couldn't.'

'You felt you should tell the father first.' It was a statement, not a question, and for a moment she didn't understand what he was getting at. And then it hit her, like a vicious body blow in the solar plexus, whitening her face to chalk and strangling anything she would have said in her throat as the pain gripped her with merciless fingers. 'Did you plan it?' he asked grimly, and now there was a very strange expression on his face that frightened her. *Did you plan it?'* he repeated in a low growl.

The shock was still so great that her vocal cords seemed frozen, but she managed a shake of her head as he rose slowly to his feet to stand looking down at her with savage revulsion.

'So it was an accident.' Dark colour stained the chiselled cheekbones, his midnight-black eyes bitter. 'On your part at least, but I have no doubt that Howard knew exactly what he was doing. He's in love with you and you presented him with the perfect opportunity. And this is our noble, holier-than-thou William, is it?'

'You've got this all wrong.' But she had left it too late to protest her innocence, and her confusion and panic didn't impress him in the least, his eyes flicking over her with grim fury.

'Sure I have,' he snarled viciously.

'I mean it,' she said desperately, trying to form coherent

words through the whirlwind in her head. 'I didn't... We haven't—'

She wasn't making much sense but he seemed to understand what she was trying to say anyway, his face contemptuous as he glared at her with narrowed, glittering eyes. 'Don't give me that, not now,' he bit out furiously. 'You knew he was crazy about you and what could happen when you ran to him for comfort. You *knew*. You lived in his home, for crying out loud, and then he visited you in Tunisia—how many times? Two, three, four? Why would he take all the time and trouble to follow you like that if you weren't having an affair? He wanted to hide you away out there, didn't he? Give himself more time to convince you you'd married the wrong man. And he's succeeded beyond his wildest expectations.'

'It wasn't like that,' she protested. Why wouldn't he *listen*?

'I could understand the way it looked to you about Gina,' Zac said tightly. 'I could even understand why you ran from me instead of staying to thrash it out—the lack of communication in your childhood and your fear of confrontation... But *this*.' He literally ground his teeth. 'I've never wanted to hurt anyone before like I want to hurt you.'

He turned then, ignoring her agonised, 'Zac, Zac, wait,' and strode up the garden without turning round, entering the house and disappearing from sight as she watched him disbelievingly.

Victoria sat in the gentle summer air for some minutes more, her senses clamouring and a beating in her head that pulsed with her heartbeat. This was going from bad to worse. Was she mad, or was it everyone else?

He thought this was William's baby. She still couldn't believe it. He actually thought that she was carrying another man's child. How could he think that—how *dared* he? The blinding confusion and hurt gave way to sheer white-hot anger. Just because he had the morals of a tom cat, how dared he assume she was the same? This was worse than anything that had gone before.

Well, she wasn't going to beg and plead for him to believe her, she told herself bitterly, her chin rising a notch and her violet-blue eyes dark with pain. He could think what he liked, and he had only married her because it had suited him to, however much he would like her to think differently now. She had been young and naive, and a virgin—a suitable mother for his future son and heir. And the merger of the family fortunes wasn't to be sneezed at either. How *dared* he act the aggrieved husband now?

By the time Victoria rose from the bench and walked towards the house she was seething with a mixture of injured pride and a deep, deep black rejection that made her soft mouth hard.

He wanted to have his cake and eat it, that was the main component of all this, she told herself as she stepped into the flower-scented conservatory and walked through into the kitchen beyond. A wife to play the gracious hostess and act as a breeding machine for the next generation of Hardings, a mistress for his pleasure. And he'd been caught out, big time.

He had had plenty of opportunity to tell her about Gina before they were married, and if his ridiculous story about Gina's mother asking him to help her daughter was true, why hadn't he explained it all at the time? And what man set an *ex*-mistress up in an apartment anyway? He must think she was a moronic half-wit, not just naive and stupid. The old cliché of what was good for the goose was good for the gander—or, in this case, what was good for the gander was good for the goose—clearly didn't sit too well with Zac's male chauvinistic tendencies. Well, she wouldn't lose too much sleep over that! she told herself bitterly.

Zac walked out of the enormous, south-facing drawing room as she entered the hall from the kitchen, his face dark and grim, but Victoria found the rage that had her in its grip provided more than enough adrenalin to face him without flinching.

'I'm going.' She made to pass him after one scathing, furious glance, but he caught her arm, swinging her round to face him.

'When I say so,' he bit out savagely. 'And I don't yet.'

'Let go of me, Zac.' She didn't struggle, standing stiff and dignified in his grasp, her face icy, and her regal composure seemed to infuriate him still more.

'Why should I? You're still my wife,' he said bitterly, a muscle moving at the side of his jaw and his handsome face stony.

'In name only.' She tried to ignore the fact that her heart was pounding like a sledgehammer at his nearness, the magnetic dark quality to his virile maleness overwhelmingly seductive even in his rage. 'That's all. It means absolutely nothing.'

Did he and Gina quarrel? The thought popped into her mind with piercing pain. Gina was a full-blooded Italian, Zac was half Italian—that made for a passionate relationship, didn't it? Latin blood and all that. And no doubt they had lots of fun making up. The thought stiffened her back still more.

'Then perhaps we ought to do something about that?' he suggested with soft venom. 'You think me the lowest of the low. I haven't got a thing to lose, have I?'

'Don't you dare touch me,' she gasped wildly as he pulled her closer, his thighs hard against hers. 'I hate you.'

'And you love the noble William,' he grated harshly. 'What an inconsistent creature you are. Or *do* you love him, Victoria?' he asked softly, his eyes lethal. 'I wonder. Shall we put it to the test? Could it be that in your desire to punish me you were hoisted by your own petard? Did he take advantage of you? Forgive the old-fashioned phrase,' he added with caustic mockery, 'because we both know you are far from old-fashioned.'

'Let go of me.' Victoria was frightened now. This dark,

angry stranger bore no resemblance to the man who had courted her with such tender passion, and who had made her wedding night a wild, sensual experience of pure ecstasy.

'You took it upon yourself to be judge and jury, didn't you, my gentle maiden?' Zac continued relentlessly, his body moving against hers as he spoke, her wrists trapped in one of his strong hands behind her back, and his other hand imprisoning her head as he held a handful of her silky soft hair in his powerful grip. 'I wasn't allowed to speak in my defence; I was hung, drawn and quartered and expelled from your life as though I was nothing. But that was your body beneath mine on our wedding night, your lips that begged me for more until you moaned my name over and over. I was there—I *know* you weren't thinking of him then.'

'Stop this. Please, Zac, stop it.' She had made up her mind she wouldn't beg him for anything again, but now she found herself doing just that. 'What do you expect from me anyway?'

'When I married you I thought it was going to be for ever, Tory. How could you do this to us?' he asked thickly.

He kissed her. Not the persuasive, passionate kisses that had always thrilled her and had her trembling and wanting more. This kiss was hot and brutal, a challenge from his hard maleness to her soft femininity, and it was ruthless in its intent.

Victoria tried to arch away, but he merely used her struggles to inflame them both, exploiting every move she made with savage determination, an unmistakable claim in his mouth and hands and body. She knew what he was doing, what he was trying to prove, but it didn't seem to make any difference to her traitorous body. It wanted him. *She* wanted him. Shock and humiliating dismay ripped through her. How could she still want him to make love to her after all she'd found out? Where was her pride, her self-worth?

'You want me.' As though emphasising her tortured thoughts his voice came low and thick as his mouth lifted from hers for one long moment, his hands now stroking over her body and her arms, freed from their iron constraint, pushing weakly at his chest. 'I could take you now—you want me, Victoria.'

'No…' It was a lie and they both knew it, to her shame.

'Yes, you want me.' His mouth took hers once more, hard and irresistibly knowing, and as she began to melt again she suddenly found herself thrust from him with enough force to make her totter backwards against the wall, her hands going out to steady herself.

'But I don't want you.' He was staring at her with narrowed, glittering eyes that pierced her soul with their contempt, his face dark and angry and his big body taut and rigid. 'Not with the smell of him about you. What sort of woman are you anyway? How could you indulge in the sort of scene you and William were revelling in at lunchtime and then respond to me like this?'

'What sort of scene?' Victoria objected vehemently, hating him, loving him. 'William had just bought me lunch, that's all.'

'Are you always that grateful when someone buys you a meal?' he asked with caustic derision. 'They must be lining up in droves if so. You're selling yourself too cheaply, Victoria.'

If she'd been holding anything she would have thrown it. 'You—'

'No labels,' he warned darkly. His eyes were black ice, and she couldn't reconcile this terrifying stranger with the man she had promised to love, cherish and honour for the rest of her life.

'I wouldn't have needed William's help if you hadn't set your mistress up in a tawdry love nest,' Victoria raged, using the weapon of attack to cover the pain that was tearing her apart. 'And you know that as well as I do. Oh, I'm not staying here to listen to any more of your accusations. I hate you. *I hate you.*'

She surprised them both with the speed with which she turned and was out of the front door, and even when the soft summer evening was shattered by his harsh, '*Victoria!*' she kept on running, her only desire to escape his dark presence.

He caught her up halfway down the short pebbled drive, and as he seized her arm, spinning her round, no power on earth could stop her hand from swinging into hard, fierce contact with his face. The sound was like a pistol shot and for a moment everything was breathtakingly still, the dying sunshine, with the fragrance of burning leaves wafting on the breeze, dappling the scene with a mellow warmth that was quite at odds with the savage emotion darkening Zac's face.

As the seconds ticked by and they remained frozen in a motionless tableau, Victoria swallowed hard. 'I'm sorry, Zac,' she said shakily after what seemed an eternity, willing herself not to compound the mistake by bursting into tears. 'I shouldn't have hit you. I know that. I...I apologise.'

He didn't say anything for a full thirty seconds more, and then his voice was quite without expression. 'I'll take you back.'

'There's...there's no need.' The urge to cry was paramount and she was fighting it with all her might. 'I can get a taxi; it's no problem.' She didn't dare look at him.

'I'll take you,' he repeated flatly. 'Get in the car.'

Victoria didn't argue further. She was feeling very strange, and the truth of the matter was that she didn't trust her trembling legs to get her any further than the few feet to Zac's Jaguar. She tottered over to the car, her head whirling.

Once he had shut the passenger door she watched him

walk round the bonnet and slide into the driving seat. He was mad. Oh, he was *mad*, Victoria thought bleakly. And the mark of her handprint was plainly visible. She couldn't believe that she had done that, that she had hit him. And it made it all the worse because she knew, no matter what the provocation, he would never raise his hand to her.

They drove in a dark, terribly oppressive silence for some miles before Victoria said, her voice very small, 'I only left my new telephone number with your secretary when I called yesterday, didn't I? The flat's in Richmond, in—'

'I know where it is,' he cut in coldly.

Of course. Her mother. No doubt her mother was desperately trying to worm herself back into Zac's good books by keeping him informed of his wife's whereabouts, Victoria thought bitterly. Coral had done nothing but command her to return to her husband since she had come back from Tunisia, and one of the reasons Victoria hadn't told her mother where she was in the initial few weeks after the wedding was that she'd known it would be instantly reported to Zac.

Her mother was far more concerned with swelling the Chigley-Brown coffers with the lucrative business deal her lawyers had set up with the Harding empire, and which her daughter's scandalous behaviour—her mother's own words—had jeopardised, than worrying about respecting her daughter's wish for solitude. No doubt Zac had known about the flat even before she had the key.

They said nothing more on the journey to Richmond, and when Zac drew into the charming little mews in which the flat was situated Victoria was out of the car before he had a chance to open the door for her, her face as white as a sheet.

'Goodbye, Zac.' He had walked round to her side, his face dark and sombre, and stood looking down at her with unfathomable eyes. She couldn't read a thing from his expression.

'Goodbye, Tory.' Somehow the 'Tory' sounded more final than anything else could have done, and in that moment Victoria knew he was *really* saying goodbye. Goodbye to his old pet name for her and all the intimate connotations it held. Goodbye to their marriage, their dreams, their hopes for the future. And she couldn't bear it. Oh, she couldn't bear it...

For a long moment the truth trembled on her lips. She wanted to tell him she had never slept with William, that he was nothing more than a friend, that she could never allow any other man access to her body or her heart. She wanted to tell him that this child she was carrying was his flesh and blood, and that she wanted it more than she had ever wanted anything in her life because it was *his*. A unique part of them both.

Something of her inward struggle must have shown on her face, because she saw the dark eyes narrow as he frowned questioningly at her. 'What is it?' he asked softly. 'What's the matter?'

But nothing had changed. She continued to stare at him as her mind raced. The reasons that had caused her to walk out on him in the first place were still there. Very much still there. Something her mother had let slip, whether by design or mistake Victoria wasn't sure, about Gina being at a social function recently along with Zac burnt in her memory.

Victoria suspected Coral had woven the juicy titbit into the conversation with the intention of making her jealous and spurring her on to fight for him—in view of the other woman's brazenness—but it had had the opposite effect.

She wasn't going to fight for him. Victoria looked up into the familiar handsome face she loved so much. If she started that now, she would end up fighting the same battle for the rest of her life. Because there was always another Gina round the corner, when the present model had departed.

If she wasn't enough for him, then it was better he

pursued the life he wanted with women who could cope with his morals and outlook. Because she couldn't. *She couldn't.* She loved him too much to share him.

And she would raise his child *her* way, she told herself with a sudden fierceness that darkened her eyes to midnight-blue. It would have her values, her principles, right or wrong. And it was probably better he didn't suspect the child was his in the long run. That way he would leave them both alone.

'What is it?' he asked again.

Now she found the strength to shake her head quickly and say, 'Nothing, nothing. Goodbye, Zac.' And she turned in one swift movement and walked across the cobbles to the front door.

This was goodbye, then. This was how love affairs ended, was it? she asked herself desperately as she fumbled blindly for her key. They had been married, she'd thought she was going to spend the rest of her life with him, and it was all gone.

She didn't look round when the door finally swung open, stepping into the house and shutting it behind her as the tears rained down her face. And then she heard the roar of his car as it left.

CHAPTER FOUR

JULY passed in a round of hot summer days and agonisingly lonely, long nights, but by the time August made an appearance—bringing a welcome change in the weather of cooler, more bearable temperatures as the heatwave ended—Victoria found she was feeling much better, at least physically. Her emotions were another story.

She was now four and a half months pregnant, and if circumstances had been different would have been relishing the fact that for the first time in her life she had a voluptuous bust, although her waistline was fast disappearing. Morning sickness had been a thing of the past for the last two weeks, and despite the misery that gripped her every waking moment she was finding she was eating like a horse. Like *ten* horses.

She glanced at herself now in the mirror as she slipped off her bathrobe and paused before reaching for her bra and pants. She didn't look too bad yet, all things considered, she thought reflectively. If anyone didn't know how small her waist was normally they would just think she hadn't got much shape, and the increased bra size was a definite improvement. Not that this happy state of affairs would last long, she reminded herself wryly. Her last visit to the baby clinic, when she had seen women of all varying shapes and sizes but all resembling slowly expanding balloons, had convinced her of that. She had no illusions.

But she didn't mind. She stared at her reflection for a moment more before reaching for her clothes and dressing slowly, her mind continuing to amble on. No, she didn't mind how fat she got—she could resemble a hippopotamus and it wouldn't worry her—as long as the baby was all right. *Oh, how she wanted this baby*. She hugged herself tight for a moment, her head drooping and her hair falling across her face in a silken shower before she straightened resolutely. And she *would* have it. Nothing would go wrong; she was young and healthy and very fit; her baby was perfectly safe. Zac's son or daughter...

She looked at the girl in the mirror, her blue eyes narrowing. She had done a lot of serious thinking in the weeks since she knew she was pregnant, a lot of growing up, and some time during that process the realisation of her own massive insecurities had dawned. But she wasn't going to let them swamp her—she was going to deal with all the dark legacies from her childhood one by one, until she had the victory over them all. She owed the child that.

And she would be a good mother. No, she'd be a *terrific* mother—she had seen the other side of the coin after all, and with Coral's example ever at the back of her mind she knew exactly how *not* to behave. This child would have love—buckets, cartloads, aeons of it—more than enough to cover its lack of loving grandparents...and a father.

Zac was suddenly there in her mind's eye and the hurt was as piercing as ever, causing Victoria to turn sharply from the mirror and walk quickly through to the small, compact kitchen, where she fixed herself a wicked breakfast of fried bread, eggs and bacon with a blithe disregard for calories.

It was just gone eight o'clock when she left the flat and the morning was a cool one for the beginning of August, the break in the hot spell causing turbulent thunderstorms that had suited Victoria just fine. There had been something incredibly galling in watching the whole of London bathing blissfully in the best July for years when she had been feeling so wretched inside.

She'd told herself she was nasty and crabby, and that just because she was so miserable it didn't mean everyone else had to be, but, nevertheless, the disappearance of all those slender, lithe girls in their gay thin summer dresses, and with attentive suitors often in tow, was a relief. Now everyone was scurrying from A to B with one eye on the weather for the next torrential downpour, herself included. It was cloudburst weather.

'Victoria?'

She had been so busy in her scurrying that she walked slam-bang into Zac before she saw him, and but for him grabbing at her arms as she ricocheted away off the pavement she would have been straight under the wheels of a number ten bus.

'Good grief, woman, what's the matter with you?' he snapped furiously, not letting go of her until she was safely on the other side of the pavement next to a solid shop front and away from the churning morning traffic. 'You're supposed to look where you're going; hasn't anyone told you? You'll get yourself killed.'

'*I'll* get myself killed?' she echoed breathlessly, glaring back at him as her anger rose in line with her colour. 'It was you who bumped into me, actually,' she challenged militantly.

Oh, he looked good—if a tame word like 'good' could be used to describe such... Her fragile equilibrium balked at continuing down such a dangerous path and she wrenched her arms from his hands, turning away from his big male bulk as she did so.

'I see. So potential wife-murderer is to be added to my list of crimes?' His tone was cool now, and carried an air of resigned contempt that suggested he held her in utter disdain.

'I didn't say that.' It had begun to rain again as it had every morning for the last week, and Victoria was belatedly aware she had forgotten her umbrella. 'Look, why are you here?' she asked tightly, aware her fine, silky hair was going to be hanging about her face in rat's tails before too much longer. He hadn't tried to see her—he hadn't even phoned—in the last four weeks since her disastrous visit to their house, and now here he was waiting outside the flat and them blaming her when he had all but hurled her into the road. And still she loved this man...

'I need to talk to you.'

It was said with such a lack of warmth that it was all Victoria could do not to cry. This was Zac, her Zac; how had they come to such a pass? But then he wasn't her Zac, was he? He was Gina's, and therein lay the root of all her misery. Gina's warm, olive-tinted face and vibrant velvet-brown eyes were on the screen on her mind, their beauty mocking her, and she dealt with her anguish by drawing herself up and making her voice as icy as his as she said, 'We have nothing to talk about. I thought I'd made that perfectly clear.'

'You returned my cheque,' Zac began irritably, and then, as the rain turned into a fierce squall that threatened to soak them, he said, his tone imperious, 'We can't talk here; this is ridiculous. My car's over there; come and get in.'

'No.' One simple little word but from the expression on his face she could have said something obscene, Victoria thought with black humour. But then people didn't say no to Zac Harding, not ever. In spite of her misery she found she was enjoying the moment.

'Victoria.' He eyed her frostily, Zac at his most dignified.

It was a clear warning, but she raised her head a fraction higher, aware the water was now dripping off the end of her nose and quite spoiling the imposing effect she had aimed for as she said, 'You are making me late for work, Zac. Goodbye.'

'There is no need for you to work in that scruffy little shop, for crying out loud!' The cool composure was gone, his face one big scowl as he took her arm to prevent her moving away.

'I happen to like that "scruffy little shop",' Victoria returned curtly. It was true—she did.

When she had first applied for the job as temporary shop assistant the day after her final showdown with Zac four weeks ago, she hadn't known what to expect, and she certainly hadn't imagined she would be offered the post that very morning when she had been invited to go along and see the proprietor.

But Mrs Bretton was small and round and friendly, and the interview had digressed into a cosy chat over a big pot of tea, with Mrs Bretton lamenting the capriciousness of her daughter—the co-owner of the flower shop—who had suddenly decided to accompany her high-flier husband to the States for three months.

'He's always nipping here, there and everywhere on business,' the middle-aged woman had confided conspiratorially towards the end of their talk, 'and frankly I think my Megan suspects he might be up to a bit of hanky panky now and again, you know? I think she wants to keep an eye on him this time with him being away for quite a while. But still, you could have knocked me down with a feather when she phoned the other night and told me I'd have to get someone to stand in for a few weeks.' She'd sighed resignedly.

Victoria had nodded sympathetically but said nothing.

'And so here I am, needing some help for a while. You do understand it would just be for the next three months until she's back?' Mrs Bretton had asked anxiously. 'Would that suit you, m'dear? I know it's not everyone's cup of tea.'

'That would be fine, really.' Victoria had tried not to sound too eager, but the job sounded tailor-made for her present circumstances. The money wasn't bad, and Mrs Bretton had already said they would work out the hours to suit them both, added to which the thought of working in the fragrant environment—which was just a stone's throw from the picturesque mews where her flat was situated—was very appealing. And when she'd explained about the baby—with Mrs Bretton cluck-clucking like an old hen and plying her with home-made fruit cake—Victoria had known she had found a friend. And so it had proved. Mrs Bretton had been heaven-sent.

'Why did you send my cheque back this morning?' Zac left the matter of her job and returned to his main grievance, but again Victoria jerked herself free, glancing at her dainty gold wrist-watch as she did so with a pointed frown.

'I really do have to go.' She looked into his angry face, the rain forming tiny sparkling crystals in the gleaming blackness of his hair, and added in a softer tone, 'I'll ring you later tonight. Will that do?' He had no *right* to look so good.

'How are you feeling?' It was flat and expressionless.

It wasn't what she'd expected him to say next, and Victoria found herself staring at him for a long moment, her mouth slightly agape, before she managed to stutter, 'I...I'm fine, thank you.'

'Are you eating enough?' he asked gruffly.

Eating enough? She couldn't stop. 'Yes, yes, I am,' she said quickly, knowing that if she didn't make a quick exit this show of concern—lukewarm though it was—was going to have her howling like a baby any moment. 'Goodbye, then...' She was backing slowly away as she spoke and he let her go without another word, his eyes dark and unfathomable as he watched her, and his hands thrust deep into the pockets of his suit trousers.

The flower shop was only round the next corner, but by the time Victoria pushed open the door—a jangling bell proclaiming her entrance—she found her heart was beating as furiously as if she had just run a marathon. Which was pathetic—utterly pathetic, she told herself angrily. It didn't make any difference.

Why hadn't he phoned her if he wanted to object to her return of his very handsome cheque? Victoria asked herself, once the morning niceties had been done away with and she was sitting at a table putting together a small basket of fragrant freesias and deep red carnations. He could have—he had her number both at home and here, and it was unlikely she'd be anywhere else. Unless he thought she was still a regular visitor to William's place? she thought suddenly, her brow wrinkling.

But no, knowing Zac, he was fully aware of both her movements and William's, and therefore he'd known William had been out of the country for the last three weeks. Perhaps he'd thought she'd slam the telephone down on him? It could be that. Or was he mellowing in his feelings towards her; was this some sort of overture? A wish to put their relationship on a more civil level?

She pulled herself up sharp, stabbing an innocent carnation so hard into the green oasis in the pretty wicker basket that it broke midway down the stem.

It didn't matter if he was mellowing, she told herself angrily—not that he was of course. A proud, intensely virile man like Zac didn't appreciate his wife getting pregnant by someone else—as he saw it. He loathed her now; she had seen it in his eyes that evening four weeks ago and nothing had changed. And *his* situation was no different of course; Gina was still very much a part of his life and no doubt would continue to be so for a good few years yet.

She had returned his cheque because she was determined to make it on her own—now and in the years ahead—but his pride didn't like that. That was all it was. He had more money than he knew what to do with, and if it appeased his conscience a little—if he had one, that was—by giving her a handout it was an easy get-out.

But she didn't want his money. Victoria stared at the somewhat bedraggled basket and knew she would have to start all over again. Mrs Bretton had been delighted when she, Victoria, had shown a very real aptitude for flower arranging. It was normally the older woman's daughter who took care of that side of the business—Mrs Bretton had confided to Victoria that she was all fingers and thumbs—but her employer wouldn't think much of the higgedly piggedly mess in front of her at this moment, Victoria thought ruefully.

She picked each of the flowers out of the oasis, cleared her mind of everything but the job in hand, and banned the image of a tall, dark, handsome man with midnight-black hair and ebony eyes from entering her consciousness again that morning.

Victoria left the shop at just after five, after an unusually hectic day that had her feeling drained and tired. The rain and wind of the morning had given way to a quiet, mellow summer evening that carried the scents of a newly washed city in its soft gentle breeze, and she stood for a moment looking up into the blue sky as the sun warmed her face, drinking in the moment.

Depression had been hovering about like a little black cloud waiting to descend on her head all day after the unexpected confrontation with Zac—it had upset her more than she would have thought possible to see him again—but now she thrust the weakness away determinedly as she began to walk home, before turning after just one or two steps and walking in the opposite direction.

She was going to buy herself a dress—perhaps two, she thought purposefully. She hadn't bought any maternity clothes yet, and she had noticed the dress she had on today was slightly tight round the bust and middle. She might be a betrayed and pregnant wife—she made no apology to herself for the indulgent self-pity—but she was blowed if she was going to be a dowdy one.

Victoria spent a surprisingly contented hour or so shopping, buying herself three new sexy lace bras—the maternity ones were monstrous and seemed more built to hold outsize melons than anything else—from a little boutique close to the flower shop, and also two cleverly designed non-maternity dresses that nevertheless hid her changing shape wonderfully well and were immensely flattering into the bargain. They made her feel like herself again.

She resisted the temptation to buy more—she couldn't really afford it and she would need warmer maternity clothes in the next two or three months anyway—but on the way home she made an appointment for the next lunchtime to have her hair trimmed in an exclusive little hairdresser's she had noticed a few days before.

One of the unexpected benefits of her pregnant stage was the wonderful condition of her hair and skin, she thought encouragingly as she turned the corner into the mews and home. Her skin—normally inclined to dryness—was dewy fresh and silky smooth, and her hair had a shining softness no artificial conditioner could have improved on. Hormones weren't all bad.

Her little pep talk to herself ended abruptly as she lifted her gaze and saw the sleek silver Jaguar parked at the far end of the mews in the tiny car park like a big cat waiting to pounce.

Zac! Her heart stopped and then raced away like a runaway horse, the beat pounding through her blood as she watched the occupant of the Jaguar open the driver's door and stretch lazily to his feet. What now? More fighting?

She watched him walk towards her in much the same way a mesmerised rabbit watched the predator who was about to attack, and it was only as he reached her side that she found the strength to make a conscious effort to pull herself together.

'I thought we'd arranged I was going to phone you tonight?' Victoria said tightly as she looked up into the dark, handsome face that haunted her days and nights.

'Wrong.' His voice was even and steady and very cool. 'You *told* me that was what you were going to do, that's all.'

Power games again. Hurt and panic churned through her chest and made her voice brittle as she said, 'There was no need for you to come here; we could just as easily have talked on the phone, Zac. I really don't see that there's any point to this.'

'There are things that need sorting.' His voice was clipped now. 'About the divorce and so on. We can't bury our heads in the sand. And I prefer to do our talking face to face.'

She didn't. Victoria stared at him, the butterflies in her stomach throwing themselves into a mad St Vitus's dance that had her feeling nauseous. It was too painful, but obviously he wasn't affected in the same way she was, and why would he be? His heart wasn't involved after all. Just his pride.

The thought tightened her mouth and put steel in her backbone, enabling her to say quite coolly, 'Very well, you'd better come in, then,' as she fetched her key out of her handbag.

'Thank you.' It was dark and ironic, but she ignored the sarcasm, opening the white-painted front door to her downstairs flat and entering it quickly as she prayed for self-control.

She hated him. She did, she hated him. How could he be so darn composed and imperturbable when every nerve in her body was screaming and twanging at his presence?

'This is very nice.'

His dark bulk filled the minute hall as she turned at the sitting-room door, and she took a deep hard breath before she could say, 'Yes, I was very lucky to find it at just the right time. My mother knows someone...'

'I don't doubt it.' Now the sarcasm was dipped in pure venom. He clearly hadn't forgiven her mother for her part in all this.

'Zac—' She stopped abruptly before forcing herself to continue. 'If...if you're going to be here for a while, couldn't we at least pretend to be civil?' Her voice shook.

'Perhaps.' He eyed her broodingly without coming any further into the flat. 'There's one thing I want to ascertain first. Did you send my cheque back because William

Howard is supporting you now?' he asked flatly, his face cold and closed.

'*No!*' Her indignation was transparently honest. 'I can take care of myself, thank you very much. I don't need William or…or anyone.' She eyed him militantly, her eyes flashing.

'A questionable comment—' his eyes moved to her stomach before returning to her face '—but we won't argue the point now.' He closed the front door behind him before taking the two steps across the hall that brought him into the pretty, slightly ultra-feminine sitting room that reminded Victoria of a chocolate box.

'When are you going to tell Coral she is going to be a grandmother?' he asked without preamble as Victoria sat down carefully in one of the deeply cushioned bucket chairs and gestured for him to do the same in the other one. The sitting room was tiny—as were the other three rooms that made up the elegant little flat—and the two chairs, a coffee table, a portable TV and small midi system with a few CDs stacked in the built-in unit that ran across all of one wall made up the sum total of furniture in the neat little room. Even then it felt crowded, especially with Zac in residence.

'I…I don't know. Soon, I suppose.' The question had taken Victoria aback. She had half expected that Zac would have already paraded his account of the result of her supposed unfaithfulness to her mother, but obviously that wasn't so.

'Why haven't you told her before this, Victoria?'

His voice was quite without expression but intimidating none the less, and again she spoke perfectly truthfully as she said, 'Because she won't be interested other than feeling annoyed at being forced to acknowledge she has reached an age where a grandchild is possible. She'll treat it as a personal affront.'

'It's not the fact that the child will be a bastard that is holding your tongue?' he asked coldly.

Oh, he was good. He knew exactly which button to press to get the maximum pain, Victoria thought bitterly. She waited a moment until she could trust her voice not to shake before she answered, 'No, it's not that. And I don't really care what she thinks.'

He nodded slowly. 'But you do intend to tell her the truth?' he asked softly. 'The whole truth, including the honourable William?'

The truth? How could she tell her mother the baby was Zac's without Coral getting right on the phone the moment she left and relating their conversation word for word to Zac? But she couldn't say it was William's either, she thought wildly. She hadn't even told William yet what Zac suspected—the other man had been sent to some skirmish or other in the Middle East a few days after her devastating row with Zac, and he had no idea he was now the honorary father of a four-and-a-half-month-old foetus.

'Victoria?' He wasn't going to let her off the hook.

'Leave it, Zac, please.' She raised tortured eyes to his narrowed black ones. 'I shan't lie to my mother if that's what you're asking.' But apart from that she didn't have a clue what to say.

He nodded again, standing for a moment more before he seated himself in the chair she had indicated. 'I take it this admirable honesty was extended to your employer too?' he asked smoothly, leaning back in the chair as though he was utterly at ease with himself and his surroundings, and crossing one leg over the knee of the other. 'Mrs Bretton, isn't it?'

It was a very male pose, and with his considerable height and breadth his dark masculinity became even more flagrant than normal, causing her breath to catch in her throat.

In the twenty-four-hours-a-day 'morning sickness' days of her pregnancy, her general discomfort had taken care of any feelings of desire more than adequately—Victoria had found that constant nausea was the greatest antiaphrodisiac there was—but since she had been feeling better she'd been horrified to find her thoughts, and certainly her dreams at night, had been nothing short of erotic at times. And all very definitely featuring Zac.

Which—in the circumstances—was incredibly humiliating, she thought bitterly. But it was his fault—he was such a lean, hard, *sexy* man, with that extra something that was indefinable but which could make any woman from the age of sixteen to sixty weak at the knees with just one glance. He was...well, he was Zac Harding. And there weren't too many around.

Victoria forced her mind away from the big powerful body, and hoped Zac would attribute her burning cheeks to distress at his sudden appearance or the awkwardness of the situation—anything but lust—and tried to make her voice as smooth as his as she said, 'If you are asking me if Mrs Bretton knows I'm expecting a baby, of course she does. The position is only temporary anyway, until her daughter comes back from a trip to America at the beginning of November.'

'And then you intend to do what?' Zac asked quietly, his narrowed eyes tight on her flushed face.

'I...I'm not sure,' Victoria prevaricated stumblingly. She wished she'd had a chance to freshen up after getting home, change her crumpled dress for one of the new ones perhaps, and renew her make-up, brush her hair... *Oh, stop it.* The voice of condemnation was loud in her head. Who are you trying to impress anyway? Do you think any amount of titivation on your part would make him want you when there's Gina—warm and passionate and very definitely not pregnant—to hand? She took a deep breath, and her voice was firmer when she continued, 'Mrs Bretton said there's the chance of a few mornings a week in the run-up to Christmas when they are usually rushed off their feet.'

'Oh, good,' Zac drawled with hateful sarcasm. 'You might even be able to have the baby in the back of the

shop and then get straight up and continue with whatever
it is you do there.'

Well, the truce hadn't lasted long. 'Now look, Zac—'

'No, *you* look, Victoria,' he said sharply, straightening
up abruptly and causing her to shrink back against the
chair before she checked herself and raised her chin, staring back into his angry face bravely. 'There is absolutely
no need for you to work; you know it and I know it. I'm
quite prepared to pay you a set amount until the divorce
goes through and the financial side of things is settled.'

'Why?' She hadn't meant to ask, but she had been
astounded when the cheque had arrived in the first place,
and now his insistence that he support her and perhaps—
if he was saying what she thought he was saying—pay
her some generous maintenance when they were divorced
was confusing her still more.

As far as Zac understood she had got pregnant by
William Howard and was going to have his baby. And
Zac Harding was not a magnanimous man at the best of
times. This just didn't make sense but she couldn't work
out what he was up to.

'Why?' He shrugged broad, powerful shoulders, and
then, as his eyes flickered, stood abruptly and walked
across to the small sash window where he stood looking
out into the quiet, sun-dappled mews, his hands resting on
the wide wooden windowsill and his back towards her.
'Because you are my wife, you are entitled by law to a
part of my estate of course,' he said flatly. 'Why else?'

'I don't want it,' she said, and now her voice was very
firm. By law? She didn't want a penny off him, not a
penny.

'That's ridiculous and you don't really mean it,' he said
flatly without turning round. 'You'll need the money.'

'It is not ridiculous, and I do mean it,' she shot back
quickly. 'We were only married for twenty-four hours, not
even that, and I don't consider myself married in the true
sense.'

'But the marriage was consummated, Victoria.' He turned, and the inflexion in his voice brought hot colour surging up into her face until it reached her hair. 'You haven't forgotten that, have you?' he taunted softly, his face hard and merciless.

'Of course I haven't forgotten.' Her voice was stiff, but the images in her mind were breathtakingly vivid. Her cheeks were burning as she recalled how it had been, and partly because of the devastating vulnerableness she was feeling, and also because of the love and hurt and pain that were making her *ache* as she looked at him, she said something unforgivable. 'But you don't have to pay me indefinitely for one night of sex, Zac.'

He was quite still for an endless moment, and then his voice was a soft snarl as he said, 'What a fool I was. I never really knew you, did I?'

She was appalled at what she'd said, but she wasn't going to admit it as she stared at him, her face scarlet.

'Is that all it was to you, Victoria? An initiation process into sex? What happened? Did you suddenly realise you had married the wrong man? Was that it? Was that why you ran to him the next morning?' Zac asked with grim control.

'It wasn't like that,' she protested shakily. 'You know it wasn't. And I only left because of you and Gina—'

'Leave Gina out of this,' he rasped bitterly. 'The facts are that you left my bed and went to his within—as you have so succinctly pointed out—twenty-four hours. You knew he was crazy about you, you've probably enjoyed the thrill of keeping the poor dumb clown dangling on the end of a string for years, and you knew exactly what would happen when you turned up on his doorstep like a maiden in distress. It's the classic come-on.'

'I *was* a maiden in distress!' It was a ridiculous turn of phrase but it didn't occur to either of them. 'And how can you say "leave Gina out of this" when you...when...?' Oh, she didn't want to cry, *she didn't*, Victoria thought wildly as her lips began to quiver so much she couldn't go on.

'*Damn it all.*' Zac had moved across the room and pulled her up out of the chair before she realised what was happening, his face black with rage as he shook her slightly. 'How can you be so many different women in as many minutes?' he growled resentfully. 'Who are you? What are you? You've turned my life upside down, you tell me black is white and white is black—'

'I don't, I don't. And don't you *dare* blame me!'

And then he kissed her, a dark, angry, savage kiss, his body as hard as steel and his arms unrelenting as he ground her into him until she could hardly breathe and her head was spinning.

Her tears were vanquished by the shock of it, by the age-old challenge his body was throwing out to hers, and, to her eternal shame, she responded like a thirst-crazed mortal being offered life-giving water as a desire that was elemental gripped her.

His tongue was firing the nerves all over her body, and now, as she began to kiss him back with total abandon, he groaned deep in his throat, his hands exploring the full ripeness of her breasts through her thin summer dress, their points hard and straining against the hindrance of the soft, flimsy material.

She felt the already overloaded buttons pop as his hands sought more intimacy, and then he had peeled back the upper part of her dress, imprisoning her arms as he did so, and moved the straps of her bra down her arms as he took the voluptuously swollen weight of her breasts in his hands, his eyes devouring her.

Victoria thought she would faint at the sensations that were shooting through her body, and then, as his mouth claimed what his hands had already aroused, she gasped helplessly.

'Zac, Zac...' She moaned his name in an agony of need.

Her legs were trembling so much she could hardly stand and she could feel the tremors that were shaking his body, and she knew that in another moment he would lower her onto the carpet and take her, right here, in the tiny sitting room. And she wasn't going to stop him—*couldn't* stop him...

And then the telephone rang. And continued to ring.

It was Zac who took control of himself first, raising his head and pulling her bra into place as he said, his voice belying his command of himself, 'You'd better answer that.'

Victoria couldn't move for a moment, her head swimming and a dizziness making her ears ring, and then she slowly straightened her dress as she walked across to the telephone in one corner of the wall unit. She had to breathe deeply for a moment or two before she could pull herself together and lift the receiver.

It took all her will-power to speak normally, but even then her voice must have sounded strange as she gave the number, because William's deep tones were anxious as he said, 'Victoria? That *is* you, isn't it? Is anything wrong? Are you all right?'

'Yes, it's me. I...I'm fine, William. I've just...I've just got in from work. It's been a long day.'

She was aware of a sharp movement behind her, and then absolute silence, but she could feel Zac's eyes burning into the back of her head as William said, 'I hope you're not overdoing it, Blue-eyes; there's no need, you know. I've said I can help out. You've had a hell of a packet these last few months.'

She had got two men trying to ply her with money—two men who were prepared to keep her—and she couldn't live with either one of them, Victoria thought with a touch of hysteria. 'No, really, I'm fine.' Please, please, William, don't prolong this now, not now of all times, she prayed silently.

'Okay.' William didn't sound convinced. 'Look, I was

just phoning to tell you I'm still in the land of the living and I'll be back in a week or two. Things are a sight more complicated than we thought here, and we're following up on a couple of leads that'll take a little more time, so don't worry—all right?'

'All right. Be…be careful, won't you?' she managed weakly. The back of her neck was reaching ignition point.

'You know me, Blue-eyes, careful is my middle name. Now, take care of yourself, and don't be afraid to ask for help if you need it. You've got plenty of good friends—use 'em if you need to,' William said softly. 'I'll call you when I get back. Goodbye for now and take it easy, okay?'

Victoria could hear what sounded like shouts in the background, along with a great deal of other noise and deafening commotion, and a sudden concern for this dear friend's safety made her voice as soft as his when she said, 'Don't take any chances, William. Promise me. A story is one thing but don't try to be a hero.'

'I promise.' There was a smile in his voice as he added, 'You've gone into earth mother role already, I can tell. I've got to go, Blue-eyes…'

'Okay, thank you for ringing,' Victoria murmured quietly. She replaced the receiver very slowly, and now the silence was profound as she turned to face Zac's tense frame. 'That was William.' It was inane, but anything was better than the deafening silence. 'He's out following up a story somewhere or other.'

'So I gathered.'

The metamorphosis into ice man was complete—his eyes were black chips of glass, his face like granite. It was chilling.

'He…he was just wondering how I was getting on—'

'I'm not interested, Victoria. Not in you, not in him. We'll let the solicitors take it from here, okay?' Zac said tightly.

She could sense the black fury that was gripping him, feel the suffocating force of it as she stared into the glittering ebony eyes, and she wasn't to know that the main nub of his rage was against what he saw as his own weakness. She only knew that she loved him, and that in this minute—if it could take that terrible look off his face and transport them back to that eternity ago when they had first met—she would forgive him anything. Gina, the deal with her mother, anything.

But he had never asked for forgiveness. The truth was stark, and bitter on her tongue. And he never would. The knowledge froze her heart and body as she watched him leave without another word, and it was only some hours later, when she lay in the chaste isolation of her narrow single bed, that the ice began to melt.

Perhaps she had needed to go through this last searing meeting? Sleep was a million miles away, and some time after midnight she flung back the tangled covers and made her way into the kitchen, making a pot of strong black coffee. She wasn't going to get any sleep tonight so she might as well indulge herself.

They had no meeting point—that was clear enough, she told herself as she walked into the sitting room without turning on the light, and stood looking out of the window into the dark mews as she sipped the fragrant coffee. And she didn't want his money; that was the last thing she wanted. Just one word of regret, one indication that he had been stupid. Was that too much to ask? The answer came back loud and clear.

Two people in different worlds. He had said he didn't know her, but she knew him even less. The consuming flood of pain and loss was almost more than she could bear, and she put the coffee mug down on the floor as she began to shake with reaction.

She had known all about the fast, jet-style lifestyle he lived—her parents had existed in the same mode, hadn't they?—but she had thought he was *different*. But perhaps that was her fault? Maybe she'd assumed things she'd had no right to take for granted? Whatever, she knew she would never, *never* open up the door of her heart or her body to Zac again.

And it was only in that dark moment of supreme desolation that she acknowledged the small flame of reconciliation she'd kept burning deep inside, and watched— dry-eyed and heartsore—as it slowly flickered, and then died.

CHAPTER FIVE

IT WAS, in fact, a full three weeks before William returned to London, and by then—at twenty-one weeks pregnant—Victoria had reconciled herself to telling her mother about her condition, knowing that, whatever Coral's reaction, it couldn't hurt her.

The main component of this new strength had come from the baby itself; Victoria had felt it kick a few days before when she had been luxuriating in a long lazy bath, and the fierce rush of consuming mother love had amazed her with its intensity. Her scan at sixteen weeks had been thrilling, when she had watched the machine glide over her wet gelled stomach and outline the tiny baby hidden deep in her womb, but the emotion that had gripped her at the feel of those strong little feet had been indescribable, outdoing the picture of the scan she kept propped by her bed.

She had seen nothing of Coral for well over a month—their last meeting had been a particularly acrimonious one—but now Victoria had made up her mind that once she had seen William, and put him fully in the picture as to Zac's assumption about the father of her baby, she would then inform her mother she was going to be a grandmother. She wasn't looking forward to it, but she'd do it. But it would be a flat statement—Coral, like Zac, could assume whatever she liked; there would be no explanations from Victoria—as long as William was happy to go along with that.

True to his word, William phoned her the evening he got back to England, and they arranged to meet for lunch later in the week when William had had time to deal with tidying up the loose ends of his assignment. So Victoria was a little surprised when, the following morning just as she was about to leave for work, William phoned again.

'Victoria?' William's voice was bemused. 'Could you tell me what on earth is going on? Your husband's informants must be first-class in keeping him up to date with my whereabouts round the globe, because at seven o'clock this morning he was all but battering my front door down.'

'Oh, William.' Victoria was mortified. 'Oh, I'm sorry.'

'Partly because of jet-lag, and possibly because I felt I was in some Alice in Wonderland world where I didn't have a clue what was going on, I let him have his say without bopping him on the nose,' William continued conversationally. 'And it transpired, when I'd calmed him down enough to accept a cup of coffee, that he'd had the idea we had...how shall I put it?...made a baby. This baby—*his* baby,' he added evenly.

'What...what did you say?' Victoria whispered, her hand going protectively over the mound of her stomach wherein Zac's child lay. This was the worst scenario she could have thought of.

'That if that was so it was some form of immaculate conception,' William said pleasantly, apparently not in the least put out by the morning's happenings. 'Victoria, the guy was turning inside out—one minute wanting to rip me limb from limb, the next demanding my assurance that I intended to look after you and the baby and face up to my responsibilities. What's going on?'

'I'm so sorry—really I am.' She should have told William yesterday on the telephone what Zac suspected; she shouldn't have decided to wait until she met him for lunch, Victoria thought desperately. The whole situation was turning into a black farce.

'Did you tell him I was the father?' The perplexed note was back in William's voice and she really couldn't blame him.

'No, no, of course not,' Victoria said hastily. 'But when

I told Zac I was pregnant it was after we'd just had lunch and he assumed, after seeing us together and my having told you first...'

'And you didn't disabuse him of the idea.' Victoria thought she detected a smidgen of condemnation in William's voice, and this was confirmed when he said, 'Blue-eyes, I'd give my eye teeth for it to be true—we both know that—but this is your husband's baby and you can't pretend otherwise. It's his own flesh and blood, and it's as much his as yours—'

'*It isn't.*' She wanted to cry, but she had done enough weeping in the last five months to last her a lifetime and she wasn't going to start again. 'He gave up all right to it when he chose to keep Gina in his life. Let them have babies if they want—' the thought was excruciating '—but this one is *mine.*'

'You are going to have to work this out with him, you know that, don't you?' William said very gently. 'All I can say is that I'm here for you, Blue-eyes, whenever you need me, but I wouldn't lay claim to another man's kid by default.'

'So Zac knows,' Victoria murmured numbly. 'He...he believed you, then? He accepted you weren't the father?'

'Yes, he believed me. I think it was something in my total gob-smacked inertia that convinced him,' William said drily.

Brilliant. Utterly, utterly brilliant. The baby gave the biggest kick so far as though in answer to her desperate thoughts. What was she going to do? He'd be so *mad*...

'I'm sorry you've been dragged into all this, William,' Victoria said slowly. 'I honestly never intended it that way. I'd made up my mind to come clean with him that day, but he was so...'

'I know.' William paused before adding, 'Do you want me to come round? I've a feeling you'll be seeing him sooner rather than later.'

'No.' It was quick and definite. 'No, I'll have to see him and explain, and then just let everything settle.'

'Hmm!' William's dry, cynical exclamation expressed what Victoria already knew at heart—Zac Harding was not a man to let anything settle. 'Call me if you need me. Is lunch still on?'

'Perhaps...perhaps it'd be better in a week or two. I'll ring you.' All this furore wasn't fair on William, especially knowing how he felt about her. She'd used him enough already, albeit unintentionally, and he had his own life to live without worrying about her. 'Goodbye for now, and...thanks for being such a good friend.'

'Bye, Blue-eyes.' There was a moment's hesitation, and then he said, 'For what it's worth, I think the guy still loves you,' and then the phone went dead.

That doesn't help, William. Victoria stared at the receiver for a full minute before replacing it gently. If Zac did still have any feeling for her beyond physical attraction—and even that would die a quick death if he saw her undressed now, she thought miserably—it wasn't the sort of love that you could build a marriage—*her* sort of marriage—on. Baby or no baby, she would tell him exactly that when she saw him next.

The opportunity came quicker than Victoria expected, within the next five minutes in fact. She was just lifting her hand to open the front door prior to leaving for work when a sharp knock outside made her jump back, her hand going to her throat. *Zac.* It had to be Zac. Only his knock could denote such angry authority.

'Good morning.' His voice was deep and smooth and controlled, but nevertheless his anger fairly crackled into the space between them as she opened the door and then gestured for him to come inside without returning the salutation. She had the feeling the morning was going to be anything but good. Victoria had backed into the hall and now fairly scuttled into the sitting room as Zac closed the door. His light grey suit jacket was unbuttoned, the pale amber shirt beneath devoid of an accompanying tie, which was unusual for Zac, but she suspected from the ruffled state of his hair that he had been running his hands through it, and probably the tie had been discarded at the same time. He was clearly in the grip of a consuming emotion, and Victoria had the nasty idea it was undiluted fury—and all directed at her.

His big, lean, broad-shouldered handsomeness had an aggressive quality to it at the best of times, but now, here in the tiny feminine flat, it was overwhelmingly intimidating, his powerful masculinity lethal. And she felt scared to death.

He went straight into the attack. 'I can see from the look on your face that you've already spoken to Howard,' he grated angrily. 'so you know I went round there today. Yes?'

'Yes.' Oh, don't be so weak and subservient, she told herself bitterly. All this is *not* your fault. It was Zac who had jumped to conclusions. But, like William said, you let him, didn't you? the voice of conscience accused probingly. It suited you for him to relinquish all rights to his child...

'Do you know the sort of hell you've put me through?' Zac growled, taking a step or two towards her and then stopping abruptly when she reacted by going white. 'And don't look like that, damn it,' he snarled furiously. 'I'm not going to hurt you. What sort of a man do you think I am?'

A furiously angry one. 'Zac, I can explain all this—'

'You told me the child was Howard's,' he ground out tightly.

'No, no, I never did.' She was gabbling, her words coming out in a frantic rush, but she had never been so frightened in her life. 'It was you who said that. You never gave me a chance—'

'He said he's never slept with you, not once,' Zac said

accusingly. 'Now I want to hear it from your lips. Is that true?'

Now he was asking her to apologise for *not* sleeping with someone else? Victoria asked herself wretchedly. Impossible relationship...

'*Well?*' the word came with the force of a bullet.

'Yes, it's true,' Victoria admitted shakily. 'But I never said—'

'And I'm the only man you have ever slept with.' As a statement of fact it couldn't have been more damning.

Now Victoria raised her head, straightening her slim shoulders as she said very simply, 'Yes, you are. Of course you are.'

Did she have any idea of how beautiful she looked standing there, Zac asked himself savagely, her hair shining like a halo of silver round her delicate, heart-shaped face in which the deep violet-blue of her eyes stood out like two luminescent pools? She looked ethereal, fragile even, and yet there had to be a heart of pure steel beating above the place where the child—*his* child—lay. She had been prepared to let him believe the baby was Howard's; she had been ruthless in her determination to shut him out of her life, out of their baby's life...

This last thought caused him to say, and harshly, 'What the hell right do you think you have in trying to take my child from me? And what makes you tick anyway? Eh?'

And now it was Victoria who went on the attack in an effort to curb her guilt and panic, her voice shrill as she cried, 'Oh, I'm so sorry it didn't go all your way, Zac! You thought you were purchasing a pretty little doll who could be brought out at all the right social occasions, didn't you, and then relegated back to whatever shelf in your life was appropriate in between times, while you enjoyed yourself with your mistress? Well, thanks, but no, thanks. I don't intend to ever take that sort of treatment from anyone again. I'm in control of my life now. *Me*. Got it?'

She still didn't look pregnant. Zac found a small part of his brain was working quite independently, aloof from the searing emotion that—for a few minutes back there in William Howard's place—had actually brought a red mist before his eyes, so intense had been his rage. She was wearing a long, loose and very pretty pale peach dress in embroidered cotton which, together with the flat brown leather sandals and wide gold hoops in her ears, made her look about fifteen.

But she wasn't fifteen. She was twenty years of age— soon to be twenty-one in October—and a married woman to boot. *His* woman. The rage flared again, narrowing his eyes and straightening his mouth into a hard grim line. 'You're coming home with me, Victoria. I've had enough of all this,' he ground out tightly.

'No way.' Her chin shot up, her shoulders going back, and as she backed a step or two away from him the morning light from the small window behind her shone through the thin cotton of her dress, emphasising that which he had been unable to see before.

'When is the baby due?' He found he had to wrench his gaze away from her stomach, and his voice was shaking.

There was a long pause before Victoria said, her voice quiet now, 'December. December the twenty-fourth.'

'A Christmas baby,' he said softly, looking into her face.

'Yes.' She eyed him warily, and then, as their gaze caught and held, Victoria was appalled at the surge of fierce longing and desire that swept over her. What was the matter with her? she asked herself with caustic self-contempt. How could she still feel this way after all that he had put her through? He had married her for his own ends; she'd been little more than a pawn on Zac Harding's chessboard, however he might like to dress it up now he had been found out. She couldn't weaken, not now.

And, as though he had been reading her thoughts, Zac's

next words were very steady and controlled but back into
the onslaught as he said, 'You might not be aware of it,
but this whole crazy mess is a direct result of the way you
were manipulated and influenced as a child. You can't
bring yourself to trust me, can you? That fear of rejection
is too strong.'

'Fear of rejection?' Victoria spluttered, unable to believe her ears. He had the nerve to twist this round and
make it all her fault? He was one of his own, she had to
give him that.

'Exactly.' His eyes had narrowed into pinpoints of
black light. 'You were pushed from pillar to post as a
child, neglected in the worst possible way, and now, if
you do what your heart is telling you to do and you listen
to me, it makes you too vulnerable. That's it, isn't it?' he
finished dominatingly.

'No, that is *not* it,' Victoria hissed, beside herself with
rage at the amateur psychoanalysis. 'Have you forgotten
that a few weeks before our marriage you set Gina
Rossellini up in her own apartment? And besides that you
and my mother conspired behind my back in this giant of
a business deal—'

'Nonsense. No one conspired about anything,' he interrupted coldly. 'You're fast developing a persecution com-
plex if you ask me.'

'How can you say that?' Victoria all but stamped her
foot in frustration. 'Two important things in your life—
two *huge* things by any standards—and you didn't mention a word to me. I was your fiancée, Zac, the person
who was supposed to be closer to you than anyone else,
and you kept things like that from me. Why would you
have done that unless it was because Gina was your mistress and you had ulterior motives for our marrying?'

'I didn't want to bother you with unimportant trivia.'

It was so outrageous that if Victoria hadn't been so
furious she would have laughed, but as she stared at him,
her eyes sparking, she forced herself to take a long hard

breath before she said, 'I don't believe you for a moment but even if that was the truth it's reason enough for the divorce to go through. I want a partner who sees me as a real woman, not a decorative appendage on the end of his arm or some little doll's head who is too shallow to discuss anything of real importance with. I want to share everything with the man I love: all his decisions, his worries, his joys, his lows. I want to be the other half of a perfect whole. I don't just want to be loved—I want to be *needed*.'

'And you think I don't need you?' Zac snapped angrily.

'Oh, I've no doubt I come from the right stock,' Victoria returned tartly, 'and that as a hostess and suitable breeding machine I would be more than adequate for your purposes. But do I think you need me? I know you don't. You're autonomous, Zac.'

There was a menacing darkness to his face that would have intimidated her even just a few days ago, but since she had felt the baby move—and it was kicking more and more each day now; she had thought it had a football in there with it last night—something in her persona had shifted. This was a *baby* inside her, a real baby, and she was going to be its mother. It would rely on her for everything, and the fiercely protective love that had been born that day told her she couldn't allow her child to be brought up in the same way she had been. She owed it that at least.

Zac's world was the same one as her parents—she knew that now—and she had been a fool to think otherwise. She didn't want her baby to grow up thinking that money could buy anything, that mistresses and affairs were a way of life, that nannies and chauffeurs and hired help had time to listen and parents did not.

'Do you seriously think I'm going to stand by and let you ruin three lives?' Zac asked grimly. 'You are my wife and this is our child. It will be brought up accordingly—'

'You can't make me stay married if I don't want to,'

Victoria said wildly, 'and you can't make me take your money either. I have a bit of my own from my inheritance from my grandmother, and that'll see me through for a year or so until I can put the baby in a nursery during the day and go out to work again.'

'Over my dead body,' he ground out viciously. 'I'm not having a child of mine living from hand to mouth, and I'll fight you through every court in the land for custody, I'm warning you now, Victoria. You won't win, I swear it.'

'And I'll fight you back,' she countered tremblingly, but the overwhelming awfulness of what was happening was making her shake visibly. 'If that's what it takes, I'll fight you back.'

'Sit down,' Zac said flatly after a long screaming moment of silence. 'This is not doing you or the baby any good.'

'No.' Pregnant or no, she was *not* being labelled the weak little woman, Victoria thought truculently. If nothing else, the last few months since her marriage had shown her she could stand on her own two feet more than adequately. The fact that she wanted nothing more in all the world than to be able to lean on someone—no, not someone, she corrected herself honestly; she wanted the impossible, she wanted Zac—and ask him to share the anxiety and moments of sheer panic that went hand in hand with the unnerving thought of caring for a new life was between her and her Maker. Zac didn't know she was scared witless at times by how she was going to cope by herself, and she would rather die than admit it to him. Especially after his threats about custody.

Black eyes glinted a warning. 'I'm not asking—I'm telling you,' Zac said grimly. 'Sit.'

'There is no need for me to sit,' Victoria protested weakly, but her shaking legs were telling a different story and after one more glance at Zac's dark face she sat—the possibility of collapsing in a little heap in front of him proving a worse option than Zac thinking he had won.

But he hadn't won, and what was more he had no right to come in here throwing his weight about, she thought militantly as she added, 'I want you to go now. I just want to be left alone; that's not too much to ask.'

'When I'm good and ready,' he answered sharply, watching her from the middle of the room—astride and arrogant—with his hands on his lean hips. 'We've things to settle here.'

'You can't bully me, Zac.' She raised her chin defiantly.

'Bully you?' he growled incredulously. *'Bully you?'*

He was as mortally offended as if she had accused him of some obscene practice, Victoria thought with a touch of satisfaction that she had pierced that thick skin just a bit. 'Yes, bully me,' she repeated firmly. 'What else do you call it when you barge into my home like this?'

'I have never "barged" in my life, Victoria,' Zac said with considerable dignity, glowering at her from his stance across the room, 'and far from bullying you I came here this morning to discuss our child. *Our* child,' he added with heavy meaning.

'We've said everything that can be said,' she countered sharply.

'Oh, no, Victoria.' It was dark and soft, and she shivered at the tone. 'We haven't even begun. Trust me on that if nothing else. No one takes what is mine, not even you.'

Her mouth had gone dry, and try as she might she couldn't stop the menacing threat in his face and voice from freezing her vocal cords as he stared at her one last time before turning abruptly and walking out of the flat. She heard the front door bang behind him with something akin to disbelief, and then, as though the noise had released her from her frozen state, she jumped up and ran to the door, sliding the bolt across with shaking fingers before sliding down the smooth wood and onto the thick, expensive Axminster carpet as all strength left her.

Victoria wasn't aware how long she sat there in the hall, dry-eyed and shaking, before she made herself rise and walk into the kitchen where she made a pot of very hot and very strong coffee.

She drank one mugful straight down so fast it almost scalded the roof of her mouth, but it provided the necessary adrenalin to make her voice firm and calm when she telephoned Mrs Bretton and told her she would be an hour or so late that morning. After kicking her sandals off, she poured herself another coffee, and was sitting on one of the tall upholstered stools in the kitchen with her eyes shut and her hands cupped round the white, gold-rimmed mug as she inhaled the fragrant aroma, when the doorbell rang.

Who on earth...? Victoria waited a moment, but then, when the bell rang again, slid off the stool and padded warily into the hall. The last thing she wanted to do at this very minute was to have to talk to anyone, but it was going to be one of those mornings, she could tell. It was probably the gas man or someone from the electricity board come to read the meter, she thought as she opened the door—whilst keeping the safety chain on this time— with a tentative, 'Yes?'

It wasn't the gas or electricity man—in fact all she could see initially through the crack was the most enormous bouquet of claret-streaked lilies and deep red roses, almost a perfect replica of her wedding bouquet. Her heart stopped and then raced on madly.

'Tory?' Zac's voice was warm and soft, and as different from earlier as it was possible to be. 'I never said I was thrilled about the baby in spite...in spite of everything.'

It was the little moment of hesitation that did it. Zac Harding *never* hesitated—hesitation wasn't in his vocabulary—and for the first time Victoria realised he was as bemused about the baby as she was. She opened the door.

'Hello again.' He was standing there with a look on his face that matched his voice, and although she knew it was stupid, and that she mustn't falter in her resolve to keep him very firmly at arm's length, Victoria melted. She just couldn't help it.

'Hello.' She managed a nervous smile as her eyes went to the flowers. 'Are these for me?' she asked shakily.

'Coals to Newcastle in view of your present job, but yes, they're for you,' Zac said softly. 'And I forgot to say how beautiful you look too—radiant in fact. Motherhood suits you.'

'Beautiful?' Her head shot up in surprise and panic. He didn't think he was going to wheedle his way back into her life with cajoling charm and flattery, did he? She might be mad, but she wasn't that mad; not with a certain flame-haired, voluptuous Italian still very definitely on the scene.

'Yes, beautiful,' Zac affirmed, his voice cool now. He had noticed the alarm bell and now changed the subject with smooth control. 'And talking of motherhood, and fatherhood,' he added wryly, 'you do realise that there are decisions to be made and I have a right to be involved in them? We have to reach some sort of compromise.'

He was too calm and reasonable all of a sudden, Victoria thought suspiciously. Compromise was another word that was foreign to this man. But... She stared at him, her mind racing—she couldn't take too many of the sort of rows they had had that morning. She wasn't like him; she wasn't tough and hard and ruthless, with a win-at-all-costs mentality and a beat-the-other-guy-into-the-ground philosophy, added to which—her heart stopped and then speeded on like an express train—she had one major handicap where her relationship with Zac was concerned. She loved him. Even after his betrayal, she loved him. More fool her.

She would never be able to live with him again—even if Gina was out of the equation the hurt and distrust had gone too deep—but if only for her own peace of mind a compromise would be best, and certainly their child would benefit if its parents were on speaking terms. She decided to meet him halfway, reaching for the flowers and inclining her head as she said, 'Come in,' her voice as neutral as she could make it. 'I can spare a few minutes.'

'Thank you.' The dry note in his voice acknowledged her lack of enthusiasm but Victoria was too tied up with her own turbulent thoughts to notice.

'Do you want a cup of coffee?' she asked him carefully once he was in the flat, his big dark presence making her tiny home even tinier. 'I've just made a pot.'

'A coffee would be very nice, thank you,' Zac said with suspect meekness as he wandered through to the sitting room.

'Sit…sit down.' She stood in the doorway and waved a hand at one of the chairs before fleeing into the kitchen, the flowers clutched to her chest, and once in the small, compact space she leant against a smart, white oak cupboard as she prayed for control.

She had to be cool and composed—matronly, she told herself feverishly as she rummaged about in one cupboard after another for a vase, finally settling on a big square water jug and plunging the base of the bouquet in without removing the Cellophane at the top of the bouquet, turning away to the coffee maker in the next moment without noticing the bouquet was moving to one side and causing the jug to tilt.

The crash the water jug made as it hit the tiled floor almost made Victoria jump out of her skin, and brought Zac shooting out of the sitting room like a bullet from a gun.

'What the…?' He took in Victoria standing amidst a sea of water and jagged glass, and his sharp, 'Don't move, stay exactly where you are,' checked any movement she might have made.

He reached her in two strides, his shoes crunching fragments of broken glass, and whisked her up into his arms before Victoria could say a word, retracing his steps to the threshold of the kitchen and into the small hall beyond where he stopped, looking down into her flushed face and making no attempt to set her down. His eyes were dark and glittering and she was mesmerised.

'I've heard of keeping the little woman in the kitchen, barefoot and pregnant, but I've never realised how impractical it is before,' he said huskily. 'With someone like you, that is. Why *won't* you wear shoes, Tory?' he asked wryly.

Her habit of going barefoot whenever she could had been a bone of contention when they were courting, especially after she had trodden on a wasp on one occasion in her mother's garden, and on another had driven a half-inch wooden splinter deep into the soft flesh at the base of her toe. He'd shouted a bit then.

'I...I don't like shoes.' He had slipped his suit jacket off during his sojourn in the sitting room, and now, held close to the soft silk of his shirt, Victoria could smell the warm scent coming off his skin and feel the prickle of body hair beneath the smooth material. 'I never have,' she added weakly.

It wasn't fair that one man could be so devastatingly attractive, so sexy, so incredibly, *broodingly* male...

'Perhaps that's why your feet are so perfect.' But he didn't look down at her feet; his eyes were seemingly locked onto the soft moistness of her lips, and then his mouth was coming closer, and closer still. And she knew she wanted him to kiss her.

Victoria shut her eyes as his mouth touched hers, but then, when the kiss ended almost before it began, the light stroking of her lips not at all what she had expected, they snapped open in surprise. That was it? she asked herself confusedly. But...

'You seem to have miraculously escaped any injury,' Zac said briskly as he set her down on the thick wool carpet. 'Now you stay here out of harm's way while I clean up. I presume there's a dustpan and brush somewhere in that hidey-hole of a kitchen?'

'I... Yes. Umm...' *Pull yourself together.* 'The dustpan

is under the sink,' Victoria managed stumblingly, hearing her trembling voice with very real disgust.

She had been in his arms, held next to that wickedly male body, and he had kissed her in much the same way he would kiss a maiden aunt, Victoria thought miserably. Perhaps her changed shape had put him off? The thought was crucifyingly painful. The cleverly cut lines of the dress with its low, low waist hid her shape wonderfully well, but he would have felt only too clearly what the dress hid. He probably thought she was fat and ungainly—repulsive even? She stood lost in a black abyss of despair.

'Victoria?' he had been talking but she only heard her name.

She came out of the dark morass of her thoughts to find Zac had cleared away every last speck of glass, and the kitchen floor was now drying and gleaming. 'Oh, thank you.' She managed a smile.

'I asked you if you had a bucket or something to stand the flowers in for now?' Zac repeated patiently. 'You can arrange them later when you've got more time.'

Fiercely masculine men like him should never do household jobs, Victoria thought, with an apology to all the feminists in the world, but the touch of domesticity emphasised rather than defused his powerful appeal, making it disturbingly dangerous. She didn't want to fancy him—there was nothing she wanted less in all the world—but she was *aching* with a desire that was hot and lustful and very, very earthy.

'A bucket?' His patience sounded as if it was wearing thin.

'Oh, yes, a bucket. Of course.' Victoria tried to take control of both the situation and her own weakness as she opened the tall narrow cupboard wherein the vacuum cleaner was housed, and reached over it to the shelf where a lone bucket—hitherto unused—was sitting. He must think she was going doo-lally!

She turned to the sink, placing the bucket under the cold

tap and turning the water on as Zac tied the big parcel he had made of the broken glass with string and wrapped it round with more newspaper before putting the whole in a big black dustbin sack.

And then she jumped for the second time that morning as Zac barked—just as she was about to lift the bucket onto the floor, 'What the hell do you think you are doing now?'

'What?' All thoughts of soft yearning vanished as she glared back into his angry face. 'What's the matter?' she snapped tightly.

'You. You're the matter. For crying out loud…' He raked back a lock of jet-black hair from his brow irritably. 'You were just about to lift that bucket out of the sink, weren't you?'

'Well, of course I was,' she retorted testily, her heart still beating a tattoo. 'I wasn't aware it could jump down all by itself.' She could be sarcastic herself when she wanted to be!

'You're *pregnant*, woman. You don't do things like sky-diving or running the London marathon, and you definitely, *definitely* don't do weight-lifting,' he said with biting derision. 'Don't you know what to avoid? Haven't you been to meetings, or whatever it is women go to at this particular time?'

'If you're referring to antenatal classes, I haven't been to any yet,' Victoria snapped back furiously. 'They start at the end of September, but I've managed quite well so far in case you hadn't noticed.' How dared he insinuate she'd put the baby at risk?

He glanced meaningfully at the black dustbin sack before placing it on the floor. 'Well, now you mention it…'

'Oh, shut up!' Victoria was too enraged to tread carefully. 'I was perfectly all right before you came round this morning as it happens, but you make me so nervous—' She stopped abruptly but it was too late. The black eyes had narrowed on her face.

'Do I? Do I make you nervous, Tory?' He sounded inordinately pleased with himself and she wanted to kick him, hard.

'Not nervous exactly.' She tried to backtrack, glancing away from him, but a hard male hand turned her gaze to meet his jet-black one and she trembled at the look on his face.

'What, then…exactly?' he asked softly.

'Zac, stop this.' She hadn't forgotten his obvious distaste at her changing shape, and it enabled her voice to sound firm, even curt. 'We're separated, that is the bare bones of the matter, and all this…bickering isn't helping me or the baby.' Oh, how could you, Victoria? How could you fall back on such a manipulative feminine ploy? her conscience screamed accusingly. Only for her to reply in the next breath, Self-preservation, that's how.

'I don't want to argue with you, Tory.' He was close, far, far too close, and the touch and taste and smell of him was all about her, causing her blood to run like liquid fire through her veins and her heart to beat so loudly she was sure he must be able to hear it. 'I want to do something quite different. Something that doesn't involve the power of speech at all.'

'Do you?' She stared up into his dark, glittering eyes, drugged by the nearness of him.

'I want to undress you, very slowly,' he said softly, 'until you're naked before me, your breasts swollen and ready for my caresses and your body aching for my touch, my lips—'

'Zac, please. Please don't do this,' Victoria interrupted weakly, fighting the dark, fascinatingly sensual images his words were conjuring up. This was manipulative, Zac at his most dangerous.

'I want to explore your mouth, enjoy it, enjoy you,' he continued relentlessly, as though she hadn't spoken. 'And then my lips will claim every part of you—every part, Tory. Here—' his hand moved gently to her throat '—and here—' a provocative finger ran lightly over her breasts that were ripe and hard in answer to his desire '—and here.' Now she shuddered helplessly as his hand moved with tantalising sureness from her breasts to her stomach, pausing slightly as his fingers splayed and caressed the swollen mound, before continuing still lower.

'Don't.' She caught his hand at the juncture of her thighs, her breathing ragged and her eyes hot and wild. 'Don't touch me.'

'Why? Because you want it so much?' he asked with cruel discernment, his voice unbelievably tender.

'No. No, I can't.' She pushed at him, the movement as ineffectual as the flutterings of a tiny trapped bird against the bars of the steel cage that enclosed it. 'I can't do this.'

He caught the desperate, agonised appeal in her voice and his hands became still, his voice losing the tender note and becoming almost flat as he said, 'You can, but you won't. But I can wait, Tory. I've got time on my side. You are my wife and you are carrying my child and you cannot fight me for ever. I know it and you know it.'

He brushed past her, reaching for the brimming bucket and emptying two thirds of the water out before he placed it on the floor in a corner, dunking the ends of the bouquet under the remaining liquid.

'This child is a Harding, Victoria.' His voice was devoid of emotion as he straightened and turned back to her. 'And when you joined your body to mine as my wife you became a Harding. You're mine—*absolutely*—as I am yours.'

'How can you say that?' she hissed disbelievingly, finding her tongue at long last. 'What about Gina?'

'Gina is family and she is also a friend, but nothing more,' Zac said evenly. 'She has been merely a friend for a long time now, before I met you, but of course you do not believe that. However, I have no intention of continuing to bang my head against a brick wall on this subject, Victoria. When you are ready to listen to me we will talk;

until then you must believe what you will.' He stared at her, his mouth straight.

The arrogance made her see red. 'Saint Zac, is that it?' Victoria asked cuttingly, her eyes burning. 'You don't fool me, Zac.'

He continued to look into her distraught face for a full thirty seconds more before turning, his voice cold as he walked into the sitting room saying, 'I've never pretended to be a saint; we both know that would be ridiculous. This is getting us nowhere, your mind is still closed, but, putting our feelings aside, the lines of communication must be kept open for our child's sake. Do you agree with that? Or would you prefer an ongoing war with no winners?'

He had collected his jacket from the sitting room and now appeared in the hall again, glancing at Victoria as she watched him from the kitchen threshold. 'Victoria?' he prompted sharply, the Italian side of him very prominent. 'War or peace?'

She shrugged wearily. 'I don't want to fight, but perhaps—'

'There is no "perhaps" about it, and, knowing you as I do, I am sure you would not deprive this baby of what is rightfully his or hers. And in the long run that's exactly what you'd be doing.'

'That's emotional blackmail,' Victoria accused painfully.

'No, that is the truth,' Zac said coolly, 'but I have come to understand that you do not always recognise the truth, even when it is staring you in the face. However—' he raised an authoritative hand, cutting off the angry reply spilling onto her lips '—I will not labour the point.'

'Oh, thank you,' Victoria snapped with as much sarcasm as she could muster. How could one lone man make her so *angry*?

''You are welcome.' And he had the audacity to smile. 'We will put it down to your delicate condition.'

'Talking of which, I'd prefer to discuss this some other time.'

'I spoke of compromise, Victoria.' Now he was deadly serious, and again she bit back the retort she had been about to make as he continued, 'I do not want you to stay here alone, and I also don't like the idea of you continuing to work. It is unnecessary and may endanger the baby. And of course it goes without saying that I would prefer you not to have any contact with William Howard.'

'Is that all?' He was unbelievable. He was, he was quite, quite unbelievable, she thought dazedly, too amazed to be angry.

'Now, am I right in assuming that you do not intend to comply with my wishes on any of those points?' Zac asked expressionlessly.

'Too right,' Victoria flashed back immediately.

'So our meeting for lunch or dinner on a regular basis—perhaps a couple of times a week, something like that, nothing heavy—whilst you insist on following your own star would seem a fairly reasonable compromise to you?' he said mildly. 'Yes?'

'What?' Victoria had the sudden nasty feeling that she had been outmanoeuvred by an expert. 'I haven't agreed to anything.'

'With a proviso that if you have any problems, of any description, it is *me* you call?' Zac added evenly.

This was not how it was supposed to go, Victoria told herself silently as she tried to gather her scattered wits together. He had never once shown any remorse about what had happened, and even, *even* in the unlikely event of his story about Gina being true he hadn't told her he was spending a good deal of money on an apartment for his ex-lover, let alone about the business deal with the Chigley-Brown faction and Coral. He hadn't talked to her, he hadn't consulted her—his secretary probably knew far more about his life than she did. Their marriage had been doomed from the start but she had been too blind to see it—he didn't want a wife, he wanted a puppet, but... Her hand went unconsciously to her stomach. There was more than the two of them involved now.

'I'm not ever coming back to you, Zac.' She hadn't meant it to sound so bald and cold but panic was uppermost again.

'I'm talking about dinner now and again, not bed,' he answered just as coldly. 'I want to keep an eye on my child, that's all.'

She was right to insist on this separation and divorce. Victoria lowered her long eyelashes to hide her expression from that piercing gaze that was able to read far too much. He could be so intimidating, so icy and distant—there were times when she wondered how on earth she had been so taken in by him during their pre-marriage days, when it had been all laughter and fun and excitement. He was like two different men in the same skin.

But she still loved him and she couldn't escape from that fact. Perhaps it was the same with all men of Zac's magnetic personality? Lesser mortals were swept into their dark, consuming orbit like faintly glowing lights round a brilliant black star, until those lesser lights burnt fainter and fainter and then eventually died altogether, drained by a force that fascinated them even as it destroyed them?

He talked about compromise, but in essence he wanted to go on just the same as he had always done without a change in his lifestyle—a wife was probably rated as less useful than his business advisors, his directors, even perhaps his secretary?

'Tory, I'm not saying I didn't make mistakes.'

Her head shot up at the sound of his voice, soft and quiet now, with that thread of dark huskiness that had always had the power to turn her knees to jelly. She stared at him, her eyes dilated and her mouth slightly open, as the knowledge that he could read her mind, sense exactly what she was thinking, brought fear to the surface. He was a formidable adversary.

'I wanted to protect you from the seamier side of life—' was he saying his relationship with Gina was seamy? Victoria asked herself silently '—and the cut and thrust of business, that's all, but maybe that was wrong,' Zac said slowly. 'You were so young when we met, numerically as well as in experience, and I didn't want life touching you with its dark side. And it can be dark, Tory, as dark as hell itself. So—' he paused, his eyes tight on her white face '—I made decisions as I saw fit.'

'I'm not a child, Zac.' Victoria didn't know where the strength was coming from to speak so dispassionately when she was a quivering wreck inside, but she was thankful for it. 'I had a very short childhood as it happens; my parents saw to that. Cats and dogs were only a step up from children in nuisance value as far as they were concerned, and I learnt very quickly to behave and think like a small adult. I don't want my child—' again her hand splayed instinctively over the mound of her stomach '—to be brought up like that. I won't have history repeating itself.'

'And you think I am like your parents, like your father?' Zac asked softly, his ebony eyes, with their thick black lashes, almost closed as they narrowed on her violet-blue ones.

'Yes. No. Oh, I don't know,' she said nervously, the hot colour coming and going in her face. 'I feel like everything has changed, everything is topsy turvy, and I don't know anything except—'

'Except?' he prompted carefully. 'Come on, Tory, talk to me.'

'Except this baby is the first person who has really needed me, just as I am,' Victoria finished painfully. 'It can't live without me, I'm everything to it and it is everything to me. It's mine and…and I won't ever let it go. It's my flesh and blood.'

'It is mine too, Tory.'

It was said gently, and his voice was soft, but the steel

thread of warning running underneath the mild words was reflected in his face. And it was true, she acknowledged bitterly. It was his.

They stared at each other for what seemed an age, and then he inclined his head towards her, his face straight as he said, 'I'll be in touch,' before opening the front door and stepping into the mews beyond. He shut the door gently without turning round.

Victoria continued to stand there for some minutes staring blankly into space, and then a determined and almost peeved kick brought her back to reality. 'What's the matter, Sweet-pea? Aren't I taking any notice of you?' she whispered brokenly, her fingers trembling as they stroked her softly rounded belly. 'That was your daddy laying down the law as usual, and he didn't even have his coffee, did he?'

She stumbled through into the sitting room, feeling as though she had been run over by a steam engine emotionally, and sat down in one of the chairs with a dispirited little sigh. She had never felt so confused and mixed up in all her life, she thought wearily. And she wasn't going to blame it on hormones either.

She loved Zac, and at times hated him with equal passion. She wanted him to have a part in his child's life, and at other times she wanted him to be at the other end of the earth and to never have the opportunity to set eyes on her baby once it was born. Now, was that normal? She shook her head at herself. She didn't know about the maternity wing of the hospital—she'd be ending up in the psychiatric ward if she wasn't careful.

The brief moment of humour helped, enabling her to rise from the chair and pad through into the kitchen where she stood staring at the massive bouquet for a full minute. Zac, oh, Zac... She didn't realise she was crying until a tear dripped onto her hand. How could you even begin to understand a man like him? One minute fire and brimstone, the next arriving on her doorstep with flowers and a winning smile that would get him anything.

Only it hadn't. And now her mouth straightened as she reached for a piece of kitchen roll and dried her eyes determinedly. And it mustn't, she told herself grimly. It wasn't just her future they were considering here—there was someone far more important than her and Zac in all of this.

She wanted the warmth and security of a peaceful loving home for her child, and if that meant living with one parent, with visits to the other, then, awful though that was, she'd do it. She would. She drew her chin down into her neck as she stared ahead doggedly. It wouldn't be easy of course, talking of which... She still had to tell her mother the good tidings.

CHAPTER SIX

CORAL took the news of her imminent grandmother status even worse than Victoria had feared, which had been pretty bad.

'You've done this just to spite me, haven't you?' Coral's red-tipped talons gripped the edge of her wine glass so tightly, the stem snapped, spilling expensive red wine over the white linen tablecloth at the exclusive little restaurant Victoria had taken her mother to. Her generosity had an ulterior motive—Victoria knew her mother well enough to gauge that Coral wouldn't dream of causing a scene at Chaucer's. Although she hadn't reckoned on the wine glass, she thought now as she watched Coral play the gracious lady while the waiter mopped up and replaced.

But once the waiter had departed Coral returned immediately to the attack. 'This is just like you, Victoria.' Her mother's narrowed, hostile gaze gave a feline appearance to her pretty face that emphasised her high cheekbones and small nose. 'You have been doing things like this since the day you were born.'

'Hardly, Mother.' Victoria kept her tone light and bantering. She had learnt through countless such confrontations over her wary twenty years of life that it was the only way to take Coral on and survive the encounter with a few nerves intact. 'I think someone would have noticed if I'd done this before.'

Her mother's thin mouth tightened and she all but bared her teeth. 'This facetious attitude does you no credit, you know that, don't you?' she said cuttingly, her eyes flashing.

'Mother, I merely told you I was expecting a baby,' Victoria retorted quietly, willing her voice not to shake.

'And what does Zac think of this? He *is* the father, I take it?' Coral rasped tightly.

'Of course Zac is the father, and he's...he's pleased.' Victoria's stomach was churning, every nerve and sinew curling and tightening, but that was normal when she was in her mother's company. She should be used to it by now, she reflected bitterly.

'So you are back with him, then.' Coral spoke as if their reconciliation might go some way to atoning for her daughter's grievous sin, her stiff body relaxing slightly.

'No, not exactly.' Victoria raised her chin a notch as she forced herself not to duck the issue. 'Not at all, actually. I...I intend to have this baby and bring it up myself. The divorce will go through as planned,' she said as evenly as she could.

'Are you mad, girl?' Coral stared at her, aghast. 'The man is a Harding; doesn't that mean anything to you? He is enormously wealthy and powerful; you'll never want for anything in your life.'

'I don't intend to discuss this with you, Mother,' Victoria said very succinctly. 'Now or ever.' She eyed her grimly.

'Don't you indeed?' Coral paused as their first course—smoked-duck salad, the house speciality—arrived.

Ever the elegant, sophisticated, well-bred lady, Victoria thought bitterly as she watched Coral coldly incline her head at the young waiter before he departed again. Didn't her mother ever get tired of acting a part? But perhaps it wasn't a part—perhaps this brittle, cold shell was all that was left of the real flesh-and-blood person her mother must once have been.

'I can see why you've been hiding yourself away these last few weeks,' Coral said tightly after taking a tiny bite of one wafer-thin sliver of meat, her eyes flicking contemptuously over her daughter. 'Too ashamed to tell me, I suppose.'

'I haven't been hiding away.' Victoria took a deep breath. This was only going to be received fractionally better than her pregnancy. 'I've been working as it happens,' she said quietly.

'Working?' Coral stared at her, utterly aghast.

'In a flower shop.' Victoria actually enjoyed the moment.

The blank silence was more telling than any show of rage, and it continued all through the trout with stuffed mushrooms, and the lemon cheesecake, right up to the moment Victoria paid the bill and the two women stepped into the warm summer sunshine outside Chaucer's esteemed brass and gold doors.

'When is this—' Coral flapped a disdainful hand in the direction of Victoria's stomach, ignoring Victoria's sharp 'Baby?' '—due?' she asked coldly, her eyes scanning the street for a taxi.

'Towards the end of December,' Victoria said flatly. She wasn't going to cry, not here in the middle of the street, she told herself fiercely. She'd told her mother now; it was nearly over. She could carry this off for a few moments more.

'I shall be holidaying in the Bahamas at Christmas.' It was said in such a way that Victoria was meant to understand her mother would have been holidaying whenever the baby was expected. She would probably continue to 'holiday' for the rest of her grandchild's life.

'Really?' Victoria ignored the undertones and forced a bright smile. 'How lovely. I'm sure you'll have a wonderful time,' she said briskly. 'You'll be staying until the New Year?'

'Yes…' Coral raised a small authoritative hand and immediately a taxi glided to a halt at the side of them, causing Victoria to reflect, and not for the first time, that her mother could summon a cab in the middle of the Sahara desert and one would instantly appear. 'Can I give you a lift, Victoria?'

It was cold and dismissive, and Victoria responded to the tone as she replied, 'No, thank you. I've some shopping to do.'

Coral nodded, a barely perceptible inclination of her head, and after offering a smooth, perfumed cheek to Victoria's lips climbed into the taxi without another word or backward glance.

Victoria continued to stand without moving as she watched the vehicle pull into the mainstream traffic, and just for a moment the raw anguish that had permeated her childhood returned in a consuming rush, causing her to feel as though she was getting tinier and tinier, shrinking away into nothing. Unloved and unlovable. It was a terrifying feeling and quite devastating.

'How did it go?'

The deep male voice just behind her caused Victoria to swing round so quickly, she almost lost her balance. 'Zac.' She stared at him in surprise, the darkness evaporating. 'What are you doing here?'

'It's a lovely Saturday afternoon and I hadn't anything much to do,' he replied easily, taking her arm and beginning to walk along the pavement. 'I thought I'd have a wander, do a bit of window-shopping, take in a few rays, you know?'

Victoria stopped dead as she turned in his hold and looked up into the handsome face. Zac Harding *always* had plenty to do—in fact he ran his life with military precision—and wandering, along with window-shopping, was anathema to his fast, hectic lifestyle. And taking in a few rays? It didn't even *sound* like him.

'You came here because you thought I'd be upset after seeing my mother, didn't you?' she said slowly as realisation dawned. She didn't question how he'd known she was lunching with Coral: Zac had more contacts than MI5 and used them just as ruthlessly.

'That was a consideration,' he agreed lightly. 'Now, we have the rest of the afternoon and the evening to enjoy. What would you like to do? I'm utterly and completely yours, dear Tory.'

The lump in her throat and tightness in her chest were preventing Victoria from speaking, and she couldn't have explained how she felt to anyone. He had thought about her. He had known how the meeting—or rather confrontation—with her mother would go, and he had been concerned about how it would affect her. She stared up at him, her eyes brimming as she choked back the tears and swallowed desperately, and when Zac said, 'Hey, come on, Tory, you know what the dragon-lady is like,' she knew he had misunderstood her reaction and thought she was upset about her mother.

Which was probably just as well in the circumstances, she told herself as he pulled her into his strong male frame for one comforting moment before they began to walk again, still without Victoria having spoken. This was Zac she was dealing with—*Zac*—and she couldn't afford to forget that for a moment. He was like a chameleon at the best of times, which was one of his greatest strengths in business, but that formidably intelligent mind and razor-sharp discernment that seized on any weakness made him a terrifying adversary. And until this thing was finally settled and the lawyers had drawn up their papers that was what he was—an adversary. She forgot it at her peril.

'My boat is moored at Henley,' Zac said softly after a few moments had ticked by. 'Do you fancy an afternoon on the river?'

'Zac...' Victoria swung round to face him again, her face troubled. 'I don't think this is a good idea.' And that was putting it mildly, she thought helplessly. He looked good—no, more than good; they had only walked a few yards along the busy London pavement, but already Victoria had noticed several young women—and some not so young—take a second look, although Zac, she had to admit, seemed quite oblivious to their wide-eyed interest and in one or two cases openly lascivious stares. It had always amazed her in the past how blatant some women could be.

But she couldn't blame them; she really couldn't, Victoria thought weakly, even as the little green-eyed monster jumped on her shoulder. Zac was dressed casually as befitted a hot summer afternoon, but his charcoal jeans and open-necked dark blue shirt showed the broodingly foreign side of his dark good looks off to perfection, his broad shoulders, lean hips and long, long legs model material. He was walking dynamite, that was the truth of it.

And she was fat. Victoria thought back to how her body had looked earlier that morning as she had got ready to meet her mother, and inwardly cringed. No wonder he had been able to walk away from her so easily earlier in the week. It wasn't surprising.

'Why isn't it a good idea?' Zac frowned darkly. 'You like the water, don't you? And the world and his wife are on the London streets this afternoon. I don't like crowds.'

But crowds were safe.

'You're not meeting anyone, are you?' His voice had changed and the frown had become more ferocious. 'Later on?'

Victoria thought about lying for one split second, but only one. The trouble was she wanted to go with him, *ached* to go with him, and on a sheer practicality scale afternoons like this would be rare—if at all—in the future. She couldn't afford cosy twosomes.

And she was his wife—legally and before God. Whatever Gina meant to him, he hadn't given the dark-eyed Italian his name... But the thought of Gina had popped the warm bubble his thoughtfulness over her mother had produced, and now she found herself glaring at him before she could control her expression.

Oh, she was a mess, she thought suddenly as she lowered her eyes. Mixed up, confused, miserable and alone, and here she was going to be a mother in another four months. And Zac was going to be a father. They'd be the *parents* of one little scrap of humanity. The thought melted her.

'Are you?' Zac pressured grimly. 'Meeting someone?'

'No.' And she *was* wearing her other expensive boutique frock, Victoria told herself reassuringly, the one Zac hadn't seen before. If she was careful how she walked and sat it hid her bump extremely well. Clothed, she didn't look too bad still.

'That's settled, then,' Zac said smoothly, temper restored.

Yes, she supposed it was, Victoria thought resignedly as she glanced at her husband's satisfied face. Zac Harding had spoken and as usual it was *fait accompli*. Oh, if only she didn't love him quite so much. Or if only he loved her more…

The Georgian town of Henley, with its fifteenth-century pubs and pretty shops, was busy and colourful when Zac's Jaguar glided to a halt close to where his boat was moored.

Victoria had been on the sports-type cruiser—which was the last word in luxury—several times the preceding summer and had loved every minute of it, but now her face was apprehensive as she allowed Zac to help her on board. The craft was spacious and roomy but a boat was a boat, and suddenly the dark, magnetic drawing power of Zac's virile masculinity was magnified a hundred times in the confined space, making it a hundred times more dangerous.

'Drink?' Victoria sat down in the saloon as Zac opened the fridge to reveal such mouth-watering delicacies as smoke salmon and caviare, and he smiled wickedly in answer to her raised eyebrows.

'Okay, so I thought you'd like a few hours on the river,' he said smoothly, dismissing the evidence of his scheming with a wave of his hand. 'Nothing wrong in that, is there?

And I always get hungry on the water. You know that, Tory.'

'And thirsty.' Victoria glanced at the bottle of vintage champagne reposing in one corner. 'But I hope you've got soft drinks, Zac. I'm not having any alcohol at the moment until the baby is born, just to be on the safe side.

'Not even one glass?' he asked persuasively. 'Half of one?'

'Not one.' She softened the refusal with a smile as she added, 'I know it would probably be all right, but I want to do everything I can to make sure the baby is okay.'

He looked at her for a long moment, and then her heart began to pound as he bent forward, stroking the palm of his hand against her cheek, his voice very soft as he said, 'This baby doesn't know how lucky it is.'

Oh, no, no, she couldn't bear this, and more to combat the wild longing and painful desire that had flared in her at his touch her voice was tart as she jerked her head away, saying, 'Hardly. I can think of more auspicious starts to life than having parents who are already divorced.'

'We aren't,' Zac said grimly, the tender expression wiped off his face as though by magic. 'Not by a long chalk.'

'As near as dammit,' she persisted defiantly.

Hell! How could she look so beautiful, so soft and vulnerable, and be so damn stubborn? Zac asked himself furiously, but he forced his voice to sound cool and calm when he said, 'Doesn't it make any difference what I think? I don't want a divorce, Tory.'

'No, I don't suppose you do,' she agreed shortly.

'What does that mean?' He kept his face bland and amiable.

'You have everything you want if we stay married, don't you?' Victoria said levelly. 'A dutiful wife, maybe a son and heir to carry on the illustrious Harding name, a lucrative business deal...' She couldn't bring herself to mention Gina's name.

'The business deal would have, and has, gone through whether we married or not,' Zac said with infuriating control. 'And I have never mixed business with pleasure, incidentally; the deal wasn't relevant to us one way or the other. However—' he eyed her angry face calmly '—I didn't bring you out this afternoon to argue again.'

'No? Well, I'm sorry if I'm not behaving in line with what the great Zac Harding had envisaged,' Victoria shot back sharply.

A muscle twitched in Zac's square jaw. 'If you weren't pregnant you'd be over my knee by now,' he said grimly.

'In your dreams.' She didn't know why she was behaving like this—she was horrified at herself—but, once started, she seemed unable to stop.

'Ah, now, my dreams are a different story,' he said silkily.

He'd done it again—metamorphosed in front of her eyes, Victoria thought helplessly, the dark, sensual note to his voice and the glittering fire in his eyes telling her all too clearly what sort of dreams Zac had indulged in. The same sort she had.

'I'm not interested in having this sort of conversation—'

But it was too late. His hands had captured her face and his kiss was deep and passionate, his tongue plundering her mouth until she heard herself moaning in answer to his desire.

'You're gorgeous, do you know that?' he was whispering hotly against her mouth. 'Sexy and prim, sensual and timid all at the same time. You turn me on, little mother. You turn me on like crazy... Kiss me, Tory. Tell me you want me; say it.'

His mouth had moved to cover her face in tiny scorching kisses, her closed eyelids, her nose, her ears, her throat all coming under his expert ministrations until she was panting and fluid in his arms. She'd always loved his kisses—he did them so *well*.

She gasped as his thumbs rubbed over her jutting nipples, his touch causing her to tremble helplessly as burning tremors of desire snaked down every nerve in her body, and he caught the gasp with his mouth, answering it with a growl of passion.

What was she doing? What *was* she doing? Victoria arched away on the Dralon-upholstered two-seater settee but Zac followed her, leaning over her quivering form as he kissed her again, his lips as sweet as honey and his caresses taking her into a liquid, golden world of pure pleasure.

'I want you, Tory. I want you so badly I can taste it.'

'You don't… I can't…'

She wasn't making sense, but he seemed to understand her incoherent mumblings anyway, kneeling astride her as he began to undo the tiny pearl buttons of her dress, his voice soothing but his hands shaking as he said, 'I do and you can, sweetheart, you can. You're mine, Tory…'

The deep red curtains in the boat's saloon had been closed when they had come aboard, and now the bright summer sunshine outside their cosy idyll cast a soft pink glow over the furnishings as Victoria jerked upright, her hands shooting out in a flailing motion that caused Zac to lose his balance and fall in a crashing heap on the floor. *Mine*. This was still all about possession, control.

Victoria scrambled to her feet, her hands clutching at her gaping dress, and then they stilled, her body stiffening, as she realised Zac wasn't moving. In fact he was ominously still.

'Zac?' She looked down at his big body, strangely vulnerable in its crumpled state. 'Zac, are you all right?' He still didn't move, and then, to her horror, she saw the trickle of blood on his forehead. *'Zac!'*

Her shriek must have done the trick, because in the next moment he stirred slightly, his eyelids flickering.

'Zac, Zac—oh, I'm sorry—what have I done...?'

Victoria wasn't aware she was sobbing out loud until a pair of dazed black eyes looked into hers, and a very un-Zac-like weak voice said, 'What the hell hit me?'

'The corner of the cupboard, I think,' Victoria managed shakily through her tears. 'Oh, Zac, I'm sorry.'

'Damn it all, Tory...' He struggled into a sitting position as she knelt at his side, her arms going to support his shoulders. 'The next time you want to say no, could you just say it? Without the physical abuse?' he added somewhat shakily.

His voice was wry, but there was a certain amount of manly embarrassment in the dry tones that made her all the more guilty. But she hadn't meant to knock him out, Victoria reassured herself hotly. Of course she hadn't. It had been an accident, that was all. She'd just reacted out of fear and panic.

'Shall...shall I call a doctor?' she asked tentatively.

Apparently it was the worse thing she could have said if the scathing glance from those jet-black eyes was anything to go by. 'No, thank you.' It was said with a hefty amount of dignity that spoke volumes about hurt male pride.

'Let me help you up,' Victoria fussed frantically. 'Please, Zac.'

She wasn't making it any better; she could tell from the way he closed his eyes for an infinitesimal moment before he said, with a remarkable lack of expression, 'I can manage perfectly well, Victoria. I've had a small bang on the head, that's all.' But then, as he rose to his feet and his face went white, her arms went round him anyway before he shrugged her off and stepped through the door into the fresh air of the large rear sundeck.

She watched him breathe deeply for a few seconds before she said, her voice quivering, 'Shall I get you a drink?'

'Please.' And his voice was more Zac-like as he added,

his tone dark and sardonic, 'And I don't want a soft drink in case you're wondering. I'll force a glassful of that excellent champagne down. They tell me there's nothing like it when you've been beaten up by the woman in your life.'

'I didn't lay a hand on you,' Victoria protested quickly, utterly mortified he was making her out to be some sort of female thug.

'I don't know if that makes it worse or better.'

It was Zac who opened the bottle of champagne, and Victoria joined him in a small glass of the delicious, effervescent wine because she felt she needed something stronger than fresh orange juice. The sight of his still body lying at her feet was something she would never forget until her dying day, she thought soberly as Zac started the engine—despite her protestation that he should take it easy for the rest of the day—and pulled out into the river. He had looked so…helpless.

Victoria was as tense as a coiled spring for the first part of the afternoon, but then, as the mellow warmth of the late summer day and Zac's easy and congenial conversation began to work its magic, she began to relax and enjoy herself.

He allowed her to clean the cut on his forehead when they stopped late in the day to eat, but he made no effort to touch her again—not that she could blame him, Victoria thought wryly—his attitude one of friendly affection and nothing more. It suited her, it was *exactly* what she wanted, Victoria told herself firmly, but still—ridiculously—it hurt.

Dusk was blazing across the sky in a river of scarlet and gold when they eventually returned to the mooring, turning the evening shadows into deep, night-washed mauve and burnt orange.

Victoria had enjoyed herself—too much—and the self-knowledge made her voice cool and stiff as she thanked Zac for the day out with a very formal little speech that made his eyes twinkle.

'The pleasure was all mine.' He smiled lazily, his big body silhouetted against the night sky.

'And...and I am sorry about what happened earlier,' Victoria added, his magnanimity putting her to shame.

'Think nothing of it.' He bent forward, so close she could smell the warm summer fragrance of his clean male skin, and kissed her lightly on the lips before straightening as he said mockingly, 'There's no gain without pain; isn't that what they say?'

'You haven't gained anything,' Victoria pointed out quietly.

'The pleasure of a day in your company?' he suggested evenly. 'I like being with you, Tory. I always have. That's gain enough.'

He liked being with Gina too.

For a moment Victoria thought she had said the words out loud, but then, when his face didn't change, she knew she hadn't voiced the cry from her heart. And it would be pointless anyway.

Some men never settled down with just one woman—look at her father. Linda Ward had been his mistress for years, and there had probably been others before her, Victoria thought a trifle bitterly. But she wasn't like her mother. There was no way she could accept or tolerate another woman in Zac's life.

'You like being with a lot of people.' It wasn't quite what she wanted to say, but the thought of another confrontation now, after the wonderful afternoon and evening they had shared, was too much. Somewhere, some time, the rows had to stop.

'No, I never have, and still less since I met you,' Zac said softly. 'But you don't believe that yet. You will believe it, but you're not there yet. But I can wait.'

'Zac, I'm not a fool.' Victoria's good intentions to part amicably went out of the window. 'And I don't think this is wise, us meeting like this. It doesn't do either of us any good.'

'Why?' The charming companion guise was slipping a bit, Victoria noted as his face hardened and his eyes narrowed. 'Are you afraid you like it too much?'

He had hit the nail right on the head, but she managed to keep all trace of it from showing in her face, her voice very cool as she retorted, 'Don't be ridiculous.'

'You're always saying that, aren't you?' Zac said reflectively. They had reached the car, Victoria leaning against the passenger door as they had spoken, and now he put a hand either side of her, not quite touching her as he leant forward again and looked hard into her eyes. '"Don't be silly, Zac. Stop. I can't, you mustn't..."'

'Don't be—' She stopped abruptly, blushing helplessly as one black eyebrow rose in derisive silent comment.

'See?' His elbows unlocked, and now his thighs were within a hair's breadth, the faint but intoxicating scent of him all around her. 'Timid Tory, always ready to retreat into that little cast-iron shell of yours where no one can touch you. But I did touch you, didn't I, Mrs Harding? You agreed to become my wife, we had one consuming night of passion—'

'Before you got out of our bed to go and see another woman,' Victoria cut in feverishly. She had to stop this right now. He could charm the birds out of the trees, but she wasn't going to be taken in again. 'Look, Zac—' she breathed in deeply, willing her voice not to shake '—I meant what I said; this is not a good idea. It serves no useful purpose and it upsets us both.'

'On the contrary, my nervous little wife, it is an excellent idea,' Zac returned mockingly, 'and don't forget our meeting like this was part of the deal. The compromise,' he added with lazy softness. 'I've made concessions, plenty. I expect you to.'

She stared at him helplessly. 'You're not being fair—'

'Fair? What's fair?' It was quick and sharp, and told her the façade of lazy mockery was just that—a façade. 'When is life ever fair, Victoria? Was your being saddled with parents who should have been sterilised at birth fair? Or my mother dying before I was even in my teens? And was it fair to have to watch my father slowly killing himself with drink because he couldn't bear to be without her?' He stood upright, his face dark.

'Zac…' She stared at him, horrified by the revelations. 'You never told me; I didn't know.'

'There is a lot you don't know about me.' Funnily enough it was the same thought that had haunted her in the early days of their separation, but this put a different slant on it.

'How…how did your mother die?' she asked softly. He had mentioned his parents were both dead in the first whirlwind days of their courtship, but somehow the conversation had never gone deeper than that. They had lived in a rosy-coloured bubble, Victoria thought fleetingly. A bubble full of wonderful trips to the theatre, dances, expensive dinners out and such like, but they had never been alone much; they had hardly ever really *talked*.

'Giving birth to my sister.' Zac's voice was calm now, even expressionless, but he couldn't hide the pain in his eyes. 'There was a problem of some kind and she went into labour weeks early.'

'And?' Victoria pressed gently. 'What happened to her?'

'Not now, Tory. I'll tell you some other time.' For a moment she felt the rebuff like a slap across the face, and then, with lightning intuition, she understood. He didn't want to alarm her.

'It's all right, Zac, I'd prefer to hear now. It won't worry me,' she said firmly. 'This baby—' she touched her belly with a splayed hand '—is going to be fine, and so am I.'

He seemed about to refuse, and then he straightened away from her so his face was in profile as he looked towards the now silent river where the odd moored boat had lights within, faint laughter carrying on the soft night breeze now and again.

'She was beautiful, my mother,' he said softly. 'Beautiful and warm and loving, but she was never very strong. She was ill for months after my birth, apparently, and the doctors warned her it would be dangerous to have another child. But she was Italian—' his tone was rueful '—and to her big families were a way of life. I don't know if she persuaded my father to try for another child when I was ten, or if it was a genuine mistake, but, whatever, she paid with her life. The baby was stillborn, and despite all my father's wealth and the best doctors in England she followed some hours later. He went crazy, insane, he was like a man possessed, and my grandparents were so worried at the time, they took me away to live with them for a few weeks, until I insisted I go back.'

Victoria found the night was splintering with her tears and she blinked them away rapidly, her eyes focusing on the dark figure at the side of her as he continued to talk, his face hardening slightly as he said, 'The rage was gone from him but with it the will to live; he didn't know if I was there or not half the time. He began to drink—a bottle, two bottles of whisky a night and then some. The human body can't take that sort of systematic abuse. I remember I didn't cry at his funeral; I think I'd done all my crying in the years before.'

She couldn't bear the picture on the screen of her mind of a young ten-year-old Zac, just having lost the mother he clearly adored and then having to watch his father draw further and further away into a twilight world where no one could reach him.

'So...' The broad male shoulders shrugged, his voice steady with the evenness that spoke of rigid control. 'I became a very rich young man at the age of seventeen, which is not something I would recommend to anyone. I had a lot of anger in me, resentment, I suppose, and I behaved very badly for a time.''

'Oh, dear.' She managed a fairly wry response although her heart was bleeding for him. What a terrible tragedy.

'Quite.' The black eyes slanted at her as his mouth twisted in a wry smile. 'But I had one or two good friends and they weren't afraid to do some straight talking when it was necessary. Anyway, the wild young man bit finished, I took stock. My father's business affairs were being run by a load of old women masquerading as financial wizards, but there wasn't one entrepreneur in the lot of them. There wasn't one guy who was prepared to take a risk or move out, and they'd lost my father tens of thousands over the years since my mother had died and he'd lost interest.'

'So you got rid of the lot of them,' Victoria stated evenly.

'How did you know?' he asked in surprise, his eyes narrowing.

'A wild guess.' She smiled slowly. 'Just a wild guess. So, I bet that went down wonderfully well?'

'How to win friends and influence people,' Zac agreed drily. 'But the clean sweep meant I started off with a bunch of people who did things my way, and I like that.' The narrowed gaze fastened on her face now, and the mocking note was back as he said, 'There are some who say I'm a megalomaniac.'

'Heaven forbid.' Her voice was equally mocking, and with an appreciative chuckle Zac opened the passenger door, settling her in before walking unhurriedly round the bonnet and sliding in himself whereupon he started the engine without another word.

They said very little on the drive back to Richmond, and Victoria wondered if Zac was regretting opening up the way he had. He was a very private man, she'd always known that, and strong, proud. He'd revealed a great deal today.

For her part, she had found the confidences about his childhood and turbulent youth had pierced that shell he had spoken of and left her feeling sad and confused with a burning desire to comfort him. Which was dangerous— very dangerous, especially as she wasn't at all sure that she wasn't being manipulated by a mind that was far more discerning—and ruthless—than hers.

It was quite dark by the time they reached Victoria's flat, and although the streets beyond were brightly lit and busy with Londoners enjoying the mellow summer evening the mews itself was quiet and still, the odd chink of light from curtained windows mingling with the old-fashioned street lamps the cobbled mews boasted.

The black velvet sky above dotted with hundreds of tiny twinkling stars, the faint scent of fresh flowers from the pretty little window boxes at every windowsill, and the overall quaint feel to the mews, was very romantic, Victoria thought warily as Zac walked with her to her front door. Had all his talk earlier been a softening-up process for this moment? Did he expect bed and breakfast to be on the cards? She wouldn't put it past him.

The thought was electrifying rather than alarming, causing her blood to surge hotly and a little humiliating ache at the core of her before she could gain control of herself.

'Goodnight, Victoria.' Zac's voice was cool and remote, his lips merely brushing hers as she looked up at him with wide, surprised eyes, and her goodbye was still hovering on her lips as he turned, walking back to the car parked at the far end of the little street with lazy, unhurried steps that were somehow an insult in themselves.

Well, that had put her in her place. She was still standing—mouth slightly agape—when the Jaguar roared off in a swirl of sleek metal, and it was another full minute more before she opened the front door and stepped into the muggy warmth of the flat, her skin warm and glowing from a day in the fresh air.

Her hunger, which was positively embarrassing these days and especially after the way she had stuffed herself at lunch and again on the boat, drove her into the kitchen in search of hot milk and chocolate biscuits, and she took them into the bathroom with her, too hungry to wait until she was in bed for the snack.

She ran herself a bath, eating the biscuits in the meantime, and after undressing lay in the warm soapy water drinking the hot milk with her eyes shut, until a pair of tiny feet reminded her she was guilty of neglect.

'Hello, Sweet-pea.' It had become a habit to talk to the baby when she was alone, and now she watched, fascinated, as her belly answered, protruding then subsiding several times. 'Are you a boy or a girl, Sweet-pea?' she asked softly. 'Not that it matters. You're strong, that's the main thing, and you'll be beautiful to me whatever sex you are or whatever you look like.'

The tears were hot and scalding and they surprised her because she didn't really know why she was crying—she had hardly ever cried in her life before she was pregnant and now she didn't seem to be able to stop. She wasn't sure if she was crying for the baby who would have to make do with her most of the time as mother and father, or Zac—the ten-year old Zac who had wrenched her heart, and the man himself who tied her up in knots every time they met.

Or perhaps her tears were for her mother, who had never known the bitter-sweet joy she was experiencing now in spite of she and Zac being parted, and who would still miss out on the wonder of grandmotherhood. Not for Coral a warm, baby-scented little bundle snuggling into her neck and a downy head against her chin—her mother would never know or understand the sheer thrill she was feeling now at her baby kicking, Victoria thought sadly.

But most of all, she admitted silently, once she had climbed out of the bath and padded through to the bedroom, she was crying for herself. *Because she wanted Zac.* She loved him and she wanted him, and she didn't want to have to bring their child up alone.

Would she have given him a second chance if she

hadn't been pregnant? she asked herself as she pulled her
nightie over her head with trembling fingers. Patiently
waited and loved him and prayed that he would change?
Hoped that he would have learnt to love her the way she
loved him, and accept that the eternal triangle had no place
in their marriage? Probably. She nodded soberly to herself.
She didn't like to admit it—it smacked of weakness—but
that was probably what she would have done.

But she didn't have that option. The baby was too important for her to risk it being brought up in a warring
home, with a mother reduced to desperation by a husband
who couldn't see his way of life was detestable to her.
She couldn't take the risk that Zac *might* change, not now.
Might wasn't good enough.

It wasn't even just his affair with Gina. Victoria
plumped down on the bed, shutting her eyes as she hugged
her middle and swayed back and forth. He would never
understand that she needed to share everything with him
and function as his partner as well as his wife and lover.

Perhaps it was the result of her lonely, isolated childhood, but she couldn't bear the thought of entering a marriage where two people pulled in opposite directions. She
just wasn't strong enough emotionally to cope with that
sort of forced isolation again.

And then the memory of Zac's face and the pain in his
dark eyes as he had talked of his own young days pierced
her through. She didn't know what was worse if she
thought about it—having an idyllic childhood until the age
of ten and then having your world fall apart, or having the
sort of upbringing she had gone through. At least she
hadn't suffered the pain of having *experienced* what she'd
always missed, unlike Zac.

She slid down under the light covers after a time, but
her mind continued to dissect each moment of the afternoon and evening, every word that had been spoken, every
gesture and action, until she thought she'd go mad.

What was Zac doing right at this moment? The thought

came from nowhere and hit her like a ton of bricks, causing her to clench her teeth and sit up sharply as her hand reached for the lampshade. She didn't care what he was doing, she told herself irritably as light flooded the room. She couldn't afford to think in this way; it was too weakening.

She was unsettled because of the day spent in his company and the things they had shared; that was all it was. She had known all along this crazy idea of spending time together wouldn't work—for her at least. It was too bittersweet, altogether too painful, although obviously he could handle it perfectly well.

Did he ever spend the night with Gina? She liked that thought even less than the previous one, and knew she had to cut the cycle before her mind continued on such a self-destructive path. A book. She'd read a book for a while, she thought determinedly. She had at least four or five she had been meaning to get into for months now.

She read for an hour or more, forcing her mind to concentrate when it jumped all over the place, but she couldn't recall what she had read when she eventually settled back down under the covers. It was some time before she drifted into a restless, troubled sleep full of nightmarish images and strange long corridors where a little girl ran and ran, frightened and alone, and when she awoke the next morning it was to the realisation that she still had a long way to go in putting Zac Harding out of her heart and her life.

CHAPTER SEVEN

VICTORIA saw Zac several times during September, and she couldn't fault his studious concern and decorum. She couldn't fault it, and by October, which blazed in with a riot of ochre, russet and crimson on the leaves of the shrubs and trees in the little park nearby where she took an early morning stroll each day, she had hardened her heart to the feeling of pain and regret that always accompanied his now distant approach.

It doesn't matter that it's all over and that he obviously finds you totally unattractive now, she told herself on a dew-drenched morning towards the end of the month as she lumbered round the square of park, the sharp smell of clumps of late chrysanthemums and the faint aroma of woodsmoke from an early morning bonfire somewhere near mingling in the air.

Zac had taken her to the cinema the night before, and it had seemed to Victoria that the building was full of lithe, slim, model-type females with ten-inch waists and small pert bosoms. And she, in spite of the concealing folds of her maternity dress which, like the summer ones, wasn't really a maternity dress at all, had felt like a giant hippopotamus waddling along at his side.

Zac, of course, had been his usual well-dressed, lean and altogether devastating self, and she had coped with her inadequacy—not to mention the sort of fierce sexual desire that no self-respecting hippopotamus should have— by hiding behind a grumpy façade that had made the evening a trial for both of them.

He had made no attempt to kiss her goodnight after walking her to her door—if the tepid pecks on the cheek

133

he had indulged in since the day on the boat could be called kisses, she thought morosely—and had walked away as though he was glad to see the back of her. Which he probably was, Victoria admitted with black humour. The front wasn't any big deal. He also hadn't said when he'd be seeing her again.

Which was fine, just fine, Victoria told herself sharply, turning in the direction of home so she could have a cup of coffee and two of the wickedly addictive chocolate biscuits she now kept a hoard of before she set out for work. This chummy, friendly thing had been his idea anyway, all part of the supposed compromise he had harped on about. If he chose to end it, that was fine—*great*—by her. She hadn't cried once in the last few weeks, and she was doing very well all round. *She was.* And when the baby was born she'd do even better—not only would she have her child to love and look after, but she could start planning the rest of her life. She would be in control then in a way she felt she wasn't now.

She was still speaking silent encouragement to herself when she arrived at work half an hour later to find Mrs Bretton in a dreadful flap, the older woman's face as red as a beetroot.

'Oh, Victoria, oh, I'm so glad to see you, dear.' Mrs Bretton almost leapt on her as Victoria opened the door of the shop. 'I don't know how it's happened, I've never done it before in my life, but I totally forgot about an order for a bride's bouquet and a box of buttonholes one of my neighbours asked for. Her daughter's getting married today—at the registry office, you know?' Mrs Bretton whispered the last few words and bobbed her head in a meaningful way, which Victoria assumed meant the girl in question was going to be another hippopotamus in a few months' time. 'And she rang me late last night to ask why I hadn't dropped the bouquet in. Well, I felt terrible, I can tell you.'

'And you said?' Victoria prompted gently.

'I made an excuse, said I was waiting for a delivery of some flowers for the bouquet, and that I'd pop it round before eleven this morning,' Mrs Bretton said breathlessly. 'Look, I've done all the buttonholes—I was here at six this morning—and I've done most of the bouquet but you know what I'm like with the arranging side. Would you finish it off? It needs your touch. And then I'll pop everything round to her if you don't mind holding the fort for a bit? I won't be all that long.'

'No problem.' Victoria looked at the bedraggled bouquet on the table in front of her and added gently, 'You go and freshen up while I see to the flowers, then.'

By twenty past nine the bouquet was transformed into something lovely, and by twenty-one minutes past Mrs Bretton was on her way out of the door. She turned on the threshold to glance back at Victoria as she said, 'I'm just going to nip and get a wedding card and a little present, some glasses or something, on my way, so expect me back about elevenish. All right, dear?'

Victoria nodded. 'That's fine, and don't rush.' It wasn't the first time she had been left in charge of the shop since she had started working for Mrs Bretton, and she was quite confident of coping with any eventuality. 'I'll get on with the order for those table decorations for Mr and Mrs Baxter's silver wedding celebration tonight, shall I, if I get a moment between customers?'

Mrs Bretton beamed her agreement. 'Lovely, dear.'

Victoria never was quite sure how the accident happened. One minute she was standing on the stepladder in the back room as she reached for an oasis—the stock in the front of the shop having run out—and the next she was lying on the floor in a tangled heap of plant pots, flowers, earth and water, with the stepladder rocking precariously above her before it mercifully steadied and became still.

The impact of the fall had knocked all the breath out of her body and for a moment she just lay there, watching the stepladder and praying that it wouldn't crash down on her. And then, as everything became still again, she felt panic as she had never felt it before. What had she done? What had she *done*?

She hurt. Everywhere she hurt, but the pain in her back, which was shooting through to her stomach, petrified her. She'd hurt the baby. Oh, God, please, please, God, no. Please don't let anything have happened to my baby, she prayed desperately. Please, please, please. I'll do anything You want, anything, but don't let the baby be hurt. How could she have been so stupid?

She continued to lie without moving, praying the sort of unkeepable promises that people prayed at moments of dire need, and then, as she heard the shop bell tinkle and the sound of footsteps and a child's voice, she called, 'Is anyone there? Could you help me, please? Come through to the back of the shop.'

The young mother and toddler were like angels from above. Whilst his mother phoned Zac on the number Victoria gave her, the little boy squatted gravely at Victoria's side, holding her hand and talking to her as if he were thirty instead of three, showing her the grazes on his chubby knees and telling her she would be all right in a little while, just like him.

Victoria had managed to sit up but that was all—every time she tried to rise to her feet the knifing pain in her back made her gasp and sink back again—but the child's chatter helped, pulling her out of the frantic spiral of fear and panic her concern for the baby had taken her into as she talked back to him.

How Zac got from his office to the shop in ten minutes flat Victoria didn't like to consider, but when she heard the Jaguar screech to a halt outside she wouldn't have been at all surprised if the siren of a police car had followed.

Within seconds he was kneeling down by her side, his face as white as hers and his voice gentle as he said,

'Where does it hurt exactly, Tory? Don't try to move, just tell me.'

She was eternally grateful that he didn't say 'I told you so' at any point during the hours that followed, and also that the consultant obstetrician at the hospital Zac took her to—who just happened to be a good friend of her husband's and was at her bedside in Casualty before she could blink—was both tactful and kind. Beyond one sharp glance of surprise when Zac explained the circumstances of the fall, Ross Goodwin didn't indicate that he found it puzzling that the heavily pregnant wife of his millionaire friend was working in a tiny flower shop in the heart of Richmond, instead of taking it easy at home.

'Several pulled muscles, along with a good deal of bruising that will make you feel as though you've been kicked by a mule by tomorrow morning,' he said cheerfully, after he had finished his examination of Victoria, and called Zac into the room. 'I'd suggest complete bed rest for a few days, and then taking it easy for a week or two. Those muscles are going to need time to heal.'

'And the baby is all right?' Victoria asked in a very small voice. 'There's no chance this could start anything off?'

'The baby's fine.' Ross Goodwin was the antithesis of Zac, being small and plump and balding, but his smile was sweet and his brown eyes gentle as he added, 'They're tougher than you think, you know, and quite ruthless in taking everything they need to make their stay in there a comfortable one.' He indicated Victoria's rounded belly as he spoke, and then said, 'But no more acrobatics, eh? You're not as agile as you used to be.'

She nodded quickly, smiling with reaction. 'Thank you, Doctor.'

'Don't worry, Ross, I'll take care of her.' Zac's voice was grim and unusually gruff, and as Victoria glanced at his face guilt and remorse were added as further coals of fire on her head. This was his baby too, she reminded herself silently, and she could tell he had been as worried as her.

Zac insisted on taking her to the car in a wheelchair despite her protestations that she could walk, opening the passenger door and lifting her inside as though she were Meissen porcelain instead of a two-ton tessie, but in spite of his gentleness it *hurt*.

'You'll pull a muscle in *your* back,' she said nervously, in an effort to lighten the atmosphere, as he pulled the white blanket he had borrowed from the hospital more snugly round her legs. And then, as he continued to lean over her, looking deep into her blue eyes, she said, 'I'm sorry, Zac. I...I wouldn't do anything to harm this baby for the world.' Her mouth trembled.

'You think I don't know that?' he said roughly. 'You need protecting from yourself, that's the thing, and I've failed miserably in that regard, haven't I? But no more, Tory.'

'This wasn't your fault, Zac,' she said quickly, her voice high with surprise. 'It was me; I should have been more careful.' And then, as she went to reach out to him, she gasped with pain and subsided back into the seat, her face draining of colour.

'I'm taking you home.'

There was an inflexion in his voice that made Victoria think he didn't mean her little flat in Richmond, and she stared at him as he straightened up out of the car before saying carefully, 'Thank you. At least with the flat all being on one level—'

'I said I'm taking you home, Tory.' His voice was crisp and matter-of-fact and very, very firm. 'And I mean home. *Our* home.'

'The flat is my home now,' she protested quickly.

'The hell it is.' He didn't raise his voice but the tone became even more staccato as he repeated, 'The hell it is,' before he shut her door, quietly but with great emphasis.

Oh, wonderful. *Wonderful.* What was she going to do?

She couldn't exactly leap out of the car and run off, Victoria thought desperately as she watched him walk round the bonnet. And if she opened the window and yelled rape, or whatever else women shouted in situations like this, who on earth would believe her after one look at her great belly? They'd give him a medal if anything, she thought with bitter black humour. But she couldn't go with him.

When Zac slid into the car Victoria turned her head to him—the only part of her anatomy she could still move without thinking she was being stabbed by a hundred red-hot pokers—but before she could even open her mouth he took the wind completely out of her sails by saying, his voice soft, 'Tory, in this one thing, please don't fight me. I'm aware you don't trust me and that you're scared to death to make any sort of commitment, but I'm just asking you to come and stay at the house until the baby is born, that's all. You can't possibly fend for yourself over the next few days, you can barely move as it is, and you're putting the baby at risk if you go back to the flat. What if you fall again and you can't get to the phone? Or you start to feel ill?'

'Surprisingly I don't intend to make a habit of it,' Victoria said stiffly, the tightness in her voice hiding the pain in her heart as she warned herself this concern was for the baby, not her—not really. 'And there is another two months before the baby is due; I can't possibly stay with you until then.'

'Apparently it's not an unheard-of practice for the wife to live with her husband before the birth of their child,' Zac said expressionlessly. 'I hear it's even considered normal in some quarters.' He glanced at her, his face implacable.

'Maybe.' Victoria's voice was tart. 'But we aren't a normal couple, are we, so that hardly applies to us?'

'What's normal?' He turned to look fully into her eyes,

his hard, handsome face unfathomable. 'It's different for everyone.'

'Zac, I'll be all right.' She took a deep breath and willed herself to be calm. 'I'm going to be very sensible and careful.'

'I know you will, Victoria.' He smiled, but it didn't reach the coal-black eyes. 'Because I shall be looking after you. Now, we can either go straight to the house if you're going to continue to be difficult, or if you are prepared to act like a sensible mother-to-be we'll call at the flat and pick up whatever you need. It's up to you,' he said pleasantly.

He had to be the most arrogant, overbearing man in the world. All Victoria's tender, warm feelings—induced by his concern and gentleness and the way he had taken care of her—had evaporated into frustrated anger and irritation. Hundreds, *thousands* of women coped alone in her circumstances—many a good deal worse off than her—and got through perfectly well, she thought savagely. Didn't he credit her with any common sense at all? Apparently not. But he was holding all the cards and he knew it.

'Well?' He started the engine, his profile imperturbable.

'I hate you.' Childish, but if she was being treated like one she might as well behave like one, Victoria thought mutinously.

'Charming.' He didn't sound as if he cared one little bit.

'I...I need some things at the flat.' As well he knew.

'Right.' He reached across to the glove compartment and pulled out a pad and pencil, handing them to her before he began to move down the hospital car park towards the exit in the far distance. 'Make a list of what you want and where it is, because when we get to the flat you are not moving out of this seat. Ross said complete bed rest and he meant it. You've had a lucky escape; don't push your luck. Okay?'

He glanced at her—one razor-sharp, swift look—when

she didn't answer immediately. 'Okay?' he pressed grimly.

'Okay,' she agreed sulkily. 'But once we get back to the flat I shall have to phone Mrs Bretton and explain exactly what happened, and say you'll pop my keys in to her some time. That scribbled note you left was cursory in the extreme.'

'Mrs Bretton was not at the top of the list of my priorities right at that moment,' Zac said sarcastically. 'And don't do that,' he added in the next instant, his voice changing.

'Do what?' She met his eyes in the mirror warily.

'Pout like that,' he said thickly. 'You're a pregnant woman who's just had a nasty fall, but I find it difficult to remember that when you purse up your lips in that way.'

Now her face was a picture of amazement and disbelief.

'What's the matter?' Again the lightning glance before he pulled out into the main road. 'Am I supposed to be made of stone now? Is that it?' he asked irritably. 'Well, I'm not.'

'No...' He wasn't seriously saying he found her physically attractive, was he? she asked herself in bewilderment. In the last four weeks she had ballooned and she was painfully aware of it. If she and Zac had been together, if she had been one half of a close and loving relationship, her changed shape wouldn't have mattered an iota. And it didn't, not really, when she thought of the miracle happening inside her body. Nevertheless...

Victoria glanced at him sideways through her thick eyelashes as her thoughts ran on. Zac could have his choice of women; she was in no doubt about that. Leaving Gina Rossellini out of the equation for the moment, he only had to click his fingers and women would be there. Beautiful, vibrant, *slim* women—women who could still move sensuously and sexily, lissom women.

She glanced down at her rotund stomach and sighed

inwardly. And here she sat, like a beached whale, and he was talking about fancying her. Was he being gallant? Her eyes narrowed in contemplation. It was possible, she supposed. It was the only answer.

By the time they had picked up her clothes and belongings, including the neatly packed case for her eventual admittance to hospital, and made their way to Wimbledon, Victoria had stiffened up so badly any movement at all made her gasp with pain.

Getting her out of the car was like manoeuvring a live sack of potatoes inch by inch—or so Victoria felt—and when Zac insisted on lifting her up into his arms again, and she heard his faint grunt, her face was scarlet and her voice strangled as she said, 'I'm...I'm sorry about this; I'm too heavy for you.'

'How can my wife and child be too heavy for me?'

His voice was low and husky, and when she looked into his face, and saw that he meant it, she had to remind herself over and over again as he carried her into the house—*their* house—that one of the reasons he had married her, probably the main reason by what she knew now, was to have a child that would bear the Harding name.

Despite her protests Zac wouldn't put her down until he placed her gently on the big king-size bed in the main bedroom, but he was panting a bit by then, and again Victoria felt hot with embarrassment and utterly tongue-tied.

She had felt in a total daze in his arms, not the least because in spite of her size, and the pain from her poor bruised body, she was fancying him like mad. No one man had the right to be so drop-dead gorgeous, she told herself resentfully as Zac straightened from the bed and raked back a lock of jet-black hair from his forehead. And he *was* gorgeous. Boy, was he gorgeous...

'Do you think a bath might relax those muscles?' He eyed her as she lay, half propped against the pillows and as tense as piano wire. 'Ross suggested heat along with the pain-killers.'

'A bath?' The thought of a warm bath was magic, and she had answered, 'Oh, yes, a bath would be great,' before it had dawned on her just what having a bath in her present circumstances would mean—namely Zac's help and assistance. But it was too late.

When she tried to backtrack, stumbling over her words, Zac's gaze was very steady and his voice cool as he said, 'Victoria, in spite of my confession earlier, I have no intention of jumping on you at the first opportunity if that's what you're thinking. You are quite safe. And I have seen you naked before if you remember.'

There was naked and naked. She stared at him helplessly. He could call her vain if he liked, but the thought of appearing in all her glory and then lying in the bath with her belly tucked under her chin was not particularly appealing. And he thought she was worried he'd be fired with uncontrollable lust! Oh, Zac, Zac... Her earlier thought surfaced. It was either heroic chivalry or he was as blind as a bat. And she didn't know which she preferred.

'Stay there and I'll run the bath.' As he disappeared into the *en suite* Victoria tried to swing her legs off the bed so she was sitting on the edge, but the pain beat her.

She wasn't even going to be able to undress herself. The awful realisation prompted more squirmings, but by the time Zac walked back into the room she had given up and accepted fate had done its worst. She was as helpless as a baby.

'Right. The bath's ready, so let's get you out of these clothes. We'll take it nice and slowly, all right?'

Zac's voice was brisk—too brisk, Victoria recognised with burning awareness; he was clearly just as embarrassed as she was, but hiding it better—and as he slipped her shoes off she said hastily, 'Could you get my bathrobe first, please. I'll have it on the bed ready to put on once I'm...undressed.'

Stripping off would be bad enough. Stripping off and then sitting there stark naked while he sorted through her belongings for her robe was unimaginable.

It took him some time to undress her. Victoria found it was virtually impossible to raise her arms above her head, and so they were a minute or two juggling her dress off. In spite of Zac's gentleness her underslip proved even more difficult. And then she was sitting there in her bra, pants and tights, and wishing the ground would open up and swallow her.

It was as he peeled her tights down her legs that the baby decided to give an almighty kick, and with Zac's head virtually on a line with her swollen belly the movement couldn't have gone unnoticed. Victoria froze but the baby had no such qualms.

'Tory...' He froze, his eyes fixed on her rippling stomach as the baby shifted around a bit before kicking again, just to let her know it was satisfied with the new position.

And then Zac's eyes lifted to meet hers, and such was the look on his face that Victoria forgot all about her embarrassment and unease, and smiled at him as she said, 'It does that all the time at the moment; it's a right little wriggle-bum.'

'It's alive. It's moving, feeling...'

She didn't mock his amazed voice of the wonder in his eyes; she simply reached out and took one of his hands, placing it on his child as it continued to move inside her.

'It's strong.' His voice was thick and there were tears in his eyes, and it touched her more than she could ever have imagined and a lot more than she would have liked. Because—whatever else had gone before—this was the real man, this was genuine. He might have had ulterior motives in marrying her, he might be ruthless and egotistical and a law unto himself, but he was her baby's father and he loved the little scrap of humanity inside her as she did. And she wished she had never come here today. Oh, she did. This was too poignant, too painful, too *real*.

'I think I need that bath now.' She tried to make her voice light and even managed a shaky smile as he stood up, still with that expression of dazed awe and wonder on his face.

He put the bathrobe round her shoulders before Victoria unclipped her bra, thanking her lucky stars that she had worn a front-fastening one that day, and as she slipped into the thick towelling folds he helped her gently to her feet, before pulling her lacy bikini briefs down past her knees after she had eased them off her thighs.

She looked down at his dark head as he did so, at the crisp black waves that showed the odd strand of silver over his ears, and wanted to weep when she thought of what might have been.

His face was studiously blank as he lifted her—stark naked— into the mass of perfumed bubbles a few seconds later, and just as expressionless when he returned some twenty minutes later and lifted her out again, enfolding her in a huge fluffy bath sheet before carrying her through into the bedroom.

This was the room they would have shared, Victoria thought suddenly as Zac placed her carefully onto the fresh, sweet-smelling covers. He didn't think he was...? Hot panic made her tactless, and she blurted, 'I don't want to turn you out of your bed, Zac. I can sleep in another room.'

'I don't sleep in here.' He had obviously switched on the electric blanket while Victoria had been in the bath because the bed was wonderfully warm and cosy. 'And I didn't expect an invitation, so don't worry.' It was cool and faintly ironic, but as she glanced at him she saw his mouth was tight.

There was another embarrassing moment when he eased her white silk nightie over her head, but at least the water had relaxed her muscles enough for her to raise her arms gingerly and help him, although she was very aware of his eyes on the heavy thrust of her breasts. And then she was in bed, with the covers tucked up round her chin and her hands clenched tensely under the duvet.

'A light lunch, and then a couple of those pain-killers Ross prescribed,' Zac said as matter-of-factly as though her being here were an everyday occurrence. 'Omelette and salad suit?'

'I...I don't want to keep your from your work or be a distraction or anything,' Victoria muttered painfully. 'I'll be fine if you want to go, really, and—'

'Victoria, you've come between me and my work and been a distraction from the first moment I set eyes on you.' Zac's voice was very dry. 'But—' he bent and lightly stroked her lips with his own, nuzzling them apart with his tongue and deepening the kiss until the liquid fire running through her veins made her fluid and worked better than any pain-killer '—moments like this make it all worthwhile.'

He straightened, his eyes mocking as they stroked over her flushed face. 'Now, lie back and relax, and let the warmth do its healing work, and I'll be back before you know it. I'll eat in here with you if you've no objection?'

He raised an enquiring black eyebrow and Victoria found her voice as she muttered, 'No, of course not. I mean yes, you're welcome...' She wasn't making much sense, she thought with burning self-disgust, but she just wished he'd *go*.

'Good.' He smiled, and it was a killer.

He didn't often smile like that, Victoria realised as Zac looked down at her for a moment more. Usually there was a touch of cynicism in the hard male face, a wariness almost, as though he was on his guard most of the time. Which he probably was, she acknowledged in the next instant. His world was fast and ruthless—no mercy asked for or given. He couldn't afford to be gentle or tender or loving...

But he had been with her. The thought jolted her physically and as she winced at the pain it caused her torn muscles Zac said, 'Lunch, and then I suggest you sleep the afternoon away. I'll go and sort out my chef's apron.'

'You wear an apron?' she asked mockingly.

And then her eyes widened, her breath catching in her throat at the vivid picture on the screen of her mind as his smile took on a distinctly wicked slant and he said, 'Sure I do. Nothing else, mind, just an apron.' He turned, walking with easy animal grace to the door, and as he stepped out onto the landing he glanced back over his shoulder, his eyes glittering, and shut the door quietly behind him.

CHAPTER EIGHT

THE next few days were bitter-sweet, but perhaps the emphasis was more on bitter, Victoria thought to herself on the morning of the fifth day, when the knife-like pains in her back had settled into nothing more than twinges and she could actually pad along to the *en suite* with only minor discomfort.

On her first day of enforced idleness Zac had had a television set installed in the bedroom—a monster of a thing that made Victoria feel she was at the cinema every time she watched it—and had bought armfuls of novels and magazines for her to read, along with the biggest basket of fruit Victoria had ever seen and a box of chocolates to match.

He had been the perfect nurse—cooking her light, appetising meals, and keeping her supplied with drinks in between, running her hot baths, massaging her aches and pains, and even washing her hair on the afternoon of the fourth day and drying it for her with her hairdryer as she sat tensely on the side of the bed.

It had been that last exercise, when added to the massages, that had convinced Victoria that come hell or high water she had to be up and about before much longer. The feel of his large firm hands stroking their way through her hair as he had sat beside her on the bed, his hard thigh against hers and the scent of him all about her, had been a form of exquisite torture. And apart from that first kiss on the day she had arrived he had given no sign—by word or action—that he was the slightest bit interested in her in a physical or romantic sense.

She knew he was working from home now—his massive study on the ground floor of the house was kitted up with all the latest electronic wizardry—and she had heard several callers come and go at various times over the last few days, but beyond the odd telephone call when he was talking to her in her room his work didn't intrude into her sphere at all. And it was unfair—she knew it was unfair; she'd told herself so over and over again along with berating herself for her gross ingratitude—but she was feeling more and more like a bird in a gilded cage.

And so, after a tasty breakfast of toast with grapefruit marmalade followed by eggs, bacon and mushrooms, Victoria washed and dressed with extreme care, moving slowly so as not to wrench the still tender muscles, and ventured downstairs before Zac's daily—a robust personage called Mrs Watts—arrived.

She had brushed her hair until it hung in gleaming feathered wisps of white-gold to her shoulders, made up her face and even applied a discreet dab of her favourite de Givenchy perfume behind her ears, but still, when she reached the hall and stood gazing around for a moment, she felt painfully gauche and nervous.

'What the hell do you think you're doing now?'

Zac's voice was irate, but the sharply defensive reply she intended to make died on her lips as she swung round and saw him, clad in a short, midnight-blue towelling robe and clearly little else, standing in the doorway of his study.

He had obviously just had a shower before coming downstairs—she remembered she had heard the telephone ring earlier when she had been dressing, and now realised it must have been a business call necessitating a trip to the study—and his thick, damp hair was curling over his forehead, giving him a faintly boyish air. But there was nothing boyish about the hard male body. Victoria found she couldn't tear her eyes away from his hairy chest, just visible where the robe gaped open, his muscled forearms and legs and powerful, broad shoulders. He was overwhelmingly, thrustingly masculine, and his virility was all the more threatening because of the self-assurance that was completely natural and quite formidable. He was a man who was completely at ease with his body.

'I can't stay upstairs for a moment longer; it's driving me mad.' She smiled brightly as she spoke, hoping she hadn't ogled him as blatantly as she feared. 'And your doctor friend *did* only say a few days in bed,' she reminded him firmly.

He nodded slowly. 'How do you feel?' He moved into the hall on bare feet and as he reached her side she caught a faint whiff of his musky aftershave and her stomach trembled.

'Fine, fine, absolutely fine.' Oh, stop babbling, Victoria, she told herself silently. Get a grip, girl. And then, more for something to say than anything else, she added, 'You've got your study round, then? No doubt it's the hub of the house?' She glanced behind him towards the open door.

'I always feel the bedroom is the hub of a house myself,' Zac murmured conversationally, 'but come and have a look if you like. It's worked out well for my purposes.'

He didn't wait for her agreement, putting a hand under her elbow and gently steering her into the large room she remembered from her pre-wedding days, but which the then owners had designated as a separate sitting room for their teenage children.

The study wasn't at all what Victoria expected. Instead of the somewhat clinical office atmosphere she had pictured when Zac had told her about all the equipment he'd had installed, it was almost cosy. A deep red, thickly piled carpet covered the floor, the same colour reflected in the long velvet drapes at the window, and floor-to-ceiling bookshelves covered one wall, complete with books. A second wall was taken up with Zac's computer and other equipment, with his desk in one corner, but it was to the roaring log fire in the deep-set, carved wooden fireplace that Victoria's gaze was drawn, and the massive sheepskin rug in front of it set between two large comfy easy chairs.

'Oh, I don't remember this room having a fireplace.' She loved real fires, she always had, although Coral had never allowed them, preferring central heating and smart gas fires for efficiency and cleanliness. 'It makes such a difference.'

'It was here but there was a big screen in front of it along with an electric fire,' Zac said quietly as Victoria moved across the room and held out her hands to the blaze. 'I suppose the Watsons didn't trust their kids not to set the house on fire.'

'No...' She nodded but didn't turn round. 'Well, I'm glad you're using it. I love real fires; I always have.'

'Tory?' As she turned to face him he took her in his arms, taking her completely by surprise, his body hard and sure against hers and his mouth hungry as he kissed her and kissed her until she kissed him back just as fiercely, relishing the taste of him.

Somehow her hands had found their way into his robe, her fingers caressing the thick tangled hair on his chest before moving up to the broad muscled shoulders that were bare and smooth under her touch. His skin was cool, cool and fresh.

'Oh, Tory, Tory, you don't know how much I've wanted this,' he murmured huskily, his hands cupping the fullness of her breasts before he took her mouth again in a kiss that was like a kind of consummation in itself. 'These last few days have driven me mad...'

She was wearing a prim, high-necked and long-sleeved dress that buttoned down the front, and it wasn't until she felt his warm fingers on her bare skin that she realised every button was undone, and that he was peeling back her bra to reveal first one heavy, swollen breast and then the other. But as his head bent to take possession of what his hands caressed she couldn't resist him, a desire so elemental as to be unstoppable drugging her senses as his lips caused her to quiver and arch in ecstasy.

Her legs were trembling so much it was a relief when he lowered her carefully onto the rug, but the brief break in lovemaking was enough for her to realise she was almost naked, and suddenly a flood of painful self-consciousness caused her to fumble with her clothing as she tried to hide her changed shape.

'Don't, don't, I'm not going to hurt you, but let me look at you at least,' Zac murmured throatily. 'You're so beautiful, so incredibly, fantastically beautiful like this.'

'Beautiful?' She shook her head, but her hands stilled. 'Zac, I'm enormous…fat,' she protested with burning embarrassment.

'No, you're beautiful,' he said again, his eyes worshipping her. 'Your skin's got a kind of translucence I've never seen before, and I can't tell you how it makes me feel to see your belly all rounded and smooth and knowing that it's my child you're carrying. When I felt it move… It's a miracle, Tory.'

This time it was Victoria who pulled his head down to hers, kissing him with a frantic kind of innocence that touched him to the core as his words unlocked a tumult of fierce emotion.

They spent a long time touching and tasting in front of the flickering fire, the thick rug soft and warm and the room shadowed and dim from the stormy, dark day outside their haven. They explored each other with uninhibited sensual pleasure, Victoria's fears of how he would react when he saw her naked long since put to rest. He *did* find her beautiful and desirable—it was there in his eyes and the gently passionate caresses of his mouth and hands—and she so needed to be loved. The last seven months had been a barren desert of pain and anguish, and after the last few days she couldn't have resisted him; it was as simple as that. The future was the future, this was *now*, and she was only human. He was her husband and she adored him.

'Zac, I want you,' she whispered at last in a trembling whisper.

They were both liquid with desire, but she had sensed the deep restraint he was putting on his own passion and understood the reason for it, but now she captured his manhood in her fingers, guiding the silken force between her thighs.

'Tory, I don't want to hurt you.' He had drawn back a little, raising himself on one elbow to look down at her, soft and smooth and flushed, stretched out in sensuous abandonment beneath him. 'It's been so long and I want you so badly.'

'I know, I know, and you won't, it's all right.' She stroked him slowly, feeling him quiver beneath her fingers and relishing the power she had over this proud, hard man as she watched him close his eyes and arch his back. And then he twisted his body round, moving her so she found herself sitting astride him with his thighs beneath hers, her rounded belly and ripe, voluptuous breasts gleaming in the glow from the fire.

She guided him into her slowly, the ache at the core of her needing his hard strength, and then she began to move, softly, sensuously, watching his face as she felt his body move and contract. She loved him, she loved him more than life itself, and she needed him. Just this once she needed to know he was all hers, that his mind and body were centred on her and her alone.

The rhythmic undulations were coming thick and strong, and, as on their wedding night, Victoria felt herself going into another world that was all colour and touch and sensation. His possession was complete, and all the more precious because of the sensitivity he had displayed—his desire to put her well-being before his own sexual satisfaction.

The peaks of pleasure went on and on, until the final

shuddering climax released a simultaneous fierce cry of release that splintered the light behind her closed eyelids into a million prisms as they moved together as one—one body, one heart-shattering fusion. And then she collapsed against him, utterly spent, and his arms encircled her, drawing her into his body.

'Zac?' It was a full five minutes later. 'Are you awake?'

He stirred, drawing her closer into the heady male warmth of him as he said, his voice soft and satisfied, 'What is it?'

'Your daily, Mrs Watts—what if she should—?'

'It's her day off.' The fire spluttered and glowed in a shower of red-gold sparks, and as she snuggled deeper he said, 'This day is ours, Tory, just ours,' echoing the poignantly sweet refrain of her heart.

CHAPTER NINE

'WHAT do you mean, nothing's changed?'

She had known it was coming, known he wouldn't like what she had to say, but nothing had prepared Victoria for the look of sheer rage on Zac's face as she faced him over the dining table.

The day had been an infinitely sweet one. They had dozed on the rug in front of the fire, Zac's body encircling her in its warmth as he had curled himself about her, until, in spite of Zac's body heat, Victoria had begun to feel chilled. And then Zac had warmed her, slowly, sensuously, until the fire that burnt so blazingly hot in the grate had been nothing to the one inside Victoria. She just couldn't believe how he could make her feel.

Like before he had been mindful of her condition, but by the time he had kissed and stroked her all over, his mouth more intimately erotic than she could ever have thought possible as it searched out her secret places, she was melting for him.

Nothing had disturbed them in their little idyll—not the fierce wind and rain from the stormy day outside as it beat on the window in wild, blustery squalls, nor the fax in the corner of the room as it bleeped and whirred and obediently laboured on, not even the answering machine, which Zac had turned down so low that the constant messages were nothing more than faint whispers.

They'd loved and laughed and then loved and laughed some more, until, as the morning had faded into afternoon, Zac had heaped more coals and logs onto the fire, and, after dressing Victoria in his bathrobe, padded into the kitchen in search of a snack for them both as naked as the day he was born.

October had changed into November during Victoria's sojourn upstairs—it had been her birthday on the thirtieth and Zac had given her a beautiful diamond pendant and matching bracelet and earrings—and by five o'clock the evening had been as dark as midnight, the storm clouds still scudding across a sky from which a timid moon gave out a thin hollow light now and again before being swallowed into oblivion.

Zac had led her upstairs slowly. She'd been tired and he'd known it, the bruised shadows under her eyes and her swollen lips bearing their own testimony to a day of love, but when he'd followed her into the bathroom it was Victoria who drew him with her into the shower cubicle, kissing him passionately as he took her in his arms.

In the weeks that followed, Victoria could never remember that day without experiencing the erotic thrill of Zac's soapy hands moving over her body, and the feel of his own hard, powerful chest and buttocks and thighs beneath her fingers as she'd washed him in turn, her fingers exploring as they stroked his wet body.

And then he'd dried her gently and massaged rich fragrant moisture cream over her breasts and the swollen mound of her stomach, moving on to her arms and legs, even her feet, before he'd slipped his robe over her again and led her into the bedroom.

'Go to sleep for a while.' He drew back the covers as he spoke, his voice soft. 'There are a couple of things I have to deal with downstairs, and then we'll eat. Do you want to go out for a meal, or shall I order something in? Indian, or Chinese maybe? Or there's an excellent Italian place opened nearby?'

'Chinese.' She smiled at him, her eyelids heavy.

'Sweet and sour? Chop Suey? Chow Mein?'

'You choose.' She couldn't believe how exhausted she felt.

'Okay.' He bent down and stroked a silky strand of hair from her cheek, his eyes as warm as black velvet as his fingers caressed the full contours of her lips before he straightened and pulled the covers more closely around her. 'Go to sleep, my love,' he said softly, his smile incredibly sweet as he gazed down at her, drowsy and flushed in the big bed, before he walked to the door.

She must have slept—she was sure she had—but some time later she was suddenly wide awake, and in spite of all the intimacies they had shared it was the look on Zac's face in those last few minutes he had been with her that brought scalding hot panic flooding into every nerve and sinew.

She sat bolt upright in the bed as the awareness of how stupid, how incredibly *criminally* stupid she had been fully dawned. She'd gone back on every promise she'd made to herself.

There was more to love than loving somebody. She shut her eyes tight, moaning deep inside her with silent despair. The person you loved had to love you back, and it had to be the right sort of love. And Zac's wasn't.

Oh, he was good at the tender endearments, and he could be thoughtful, gentle—incredibly gentle for such a big man, Victoria thought sickly. But that extra something—the something that meant commitment, heart-and-body commitment—just wasn't in his psyche. And she'd known that; she had no excuse.

So...knowing it—why had she made love with him? Before she was married she had had the excuse of not knowing what he was really like, but she couldn't hide behind that convenient get-out clause now. When he had looked at her before he'd left the room, when he had stroked her face and smiled at her with those glittering black eyes—she could have believed she was the only woman in the world for him. And that was what he wanted her to believe; that was how he was. He probably made each woman feel special and loved; he couldn't help it.

She had been brought up in the home of a man who couldn't fully commit himself to his wife and family, and it had been hell on earth. Oh, she wasn't saying it was all her father's fault, Victoria told herself as she lay back against the pillows and opened her eyes, staring into the darkness as her thoughts sped on. Her parents' strange marriage had suited her mother, she had no doubt about that, and if Zac had chosen someone like Coral no doubt he could have lived perfectly happily with her—and she with him—while they both pursued their own lives.

But she didn't want that. Perhaps what she was looking for didn't even exist, perhaps no one was capable of remaining faithful to one person for the rest of their lives? Her childhood had been so isolated, so devoid of emotional contact, that she could accept she didn't have the first idea about how real families ticked and what went on behind closed doors.

But she did know her own limitations and what she could bear—and she *couldn't* bear watching Zac have a series of liaisons down the years, any more than she could stomach being shut out of certain parts of his life when it suited him—like his work, or his friendships, or whatever.

If her view of marriage was an impossible, idealistic dream, then so be it, but she wasn't going to put herself, and any children she might have, through the torture of living in an unhappy home. She *had* to remain strong, and she must make it clear to Zac tonight that today was just a one-off and never to be repeated, and that nothing, *nothing* had changed.

'Well?' Zac's sharp question brought her back to the present. His voice was icy, his black eyes narrowed on her pale face. 'I asked you a question, Victoria. How can you sit there and tell me nothing has changed after today?'

'Because it hasn't.' The wonderful array of Chinese food on the table was getting cold, but neither of them noticed. 'I—' Her voice faltered, but she owed him this at least, Victoria told herself miserably as she forced herself to go on. 'I do love you, Zac—I've always loved you and I probably always will—but I can't live with you. We...we're too different—'

'We're damn well not,' he growled furiously, and then, as she continued to look at him with drowning, tragic eyes, his voice was softer as he continued, 'We're not, Tory, don't you see? I love you—you must know that I love you? And you love me; you just said so. What else matters?'

That was it in a nutshell. She stared at him as his words registered in her brain. He thought loving each other was enough, but it wasn't. Her parents must have loved each other once—everyone loved each other once, she thought feverishly, before the rot set in. But love would fade and die without heart commitment.

'Lots else matters,' she answered at last, her voice quiet and painful. 'Things like Gina matter; you using me to further your business interests—'

'Right, let's clear this up now once and for all,' Zac barked sharply, clearly at the end of his tether with the way the conversation was going as he left his chair opposite her and came to sit right beside her, but his voice was controlled again when he said, 'Just listen to me without interrupting for once, right?'

She nodded, knowing nothing he could say or do would alter her mind. It was too late. It had actually always been too late.

'I admit it was pretty stupid of me to go to Gina's room without explaining what was happening first,' Zac said evenly, holding her eyes with his own, 'but I didn't want anything to spoil what had been a—' he searched for the right word and found it '—an unimaginable night of love.'

Victoria shifted restlessly but said nothing.

'Gina and I had had a relationship as you know,' he continued steadily, 'but it had ended months before I met you. We'd finished as friends—perhaps we'd been friends all along and should never have taken it that step further, because that certain something was never there, not really. Anyway, when she needed me, I couldn't turn my back on her.'

She didn't want to hear this; it wasn't helping.

'She had been ill for some time and just lost her job, which was why I helped her out with the apartment when my aunt contacted me, and on the morning of our wedding she had had the results of some test she'd gone for the week before. They were positive. She has a serious illness that needs long-term treatment which will be unpleasant, and she has no money and no close friends, besides me. She panicked, it was as simple as that, and took a load of pills without really thinking about it. And then...' He shrugged. 'You know the rest,' he said flatly.

'She called you and you went to her,' Victoria said slowly.

'And I'd do the same again,' Zac said without flinching, 'but the only thing I'd do differently is take you with me. I was trying to protect you from it all, Tory, and—'

'Treat me like a baby?' Victoria asked flatly. 'You've never shared anything with me, Zac, not really—the deal with my mother, Gina, everything. All the time we were dating we never really *talked*, and I realise now we were never alone together—'

'I wanted to be alone with you,' Zac interrupted tightly. 'Hell, how I wanted to be alone with you. But you were like the song—sweet sixteen and never been kissed—and you were so shy, so vulnerable. I couldn't believe it when I met you—I didn't think girls like you existed any more—but then I realised you were real and I was terrified I'd do something, say something, to frighten you away. I'm a man of thirty-five, Tory, and I'd been used to a fairly active sex life before I met you. I used to *ache* to have you, I tell you that now. The times I wanted to ravish you then and there are without number, but I wanted to do something right for once. And so I decided there was safety in numbers; it was as simple as that.'

'But...but we could have got to know each other better—just talked; we needn't have made love,' Victoria protested softly.

'It was too much of a risk,' Zac stated flatly. 'I didn't trust myself not to seduce you; that's how it was, Tory.'

She stared at him, not knowing what to believe. 'Zac—'

'But I couldn't wait either,' he continued quickly when she would have spoken. 'And so I rushed you down the aisle, didn't I, like there was no tomorrow? And I knew I was rushing you, Tory; I have no excuse. I knew you were the only woman I'd ever want, you see—like my mother had been the only one for my father—and I couldn't risk losing you.'

'You didn't trust me.' It was a painful little statement, but he didn't duck it, nodding slowly as he stared into her eyes.

'I don't suppose I did,' he admitted quietly, 'although it was more that I didn't acknowledge you were a grown, mature woman if anything. And I couldn't believe my luck either—that you would love *me*, marry *me*. I've done so much, seen so much, and you were so pure, so innocent...'

She continued to sit quietly, her eyes enormous as she stared into the dark, handsome face so close to hers. She wanted to believe him, believe it was really as simple as he was saying, but she didn't. She hadn't been brought up on happy endings.

'The merger was your mother's idea, and the benefit was all on her side,' Zac said slowly after a full minute had ticked by. 'It was immaterial to me whether it went through or not.'

She nodded. She believed him on that at least. It was so like Coral to cash in where she could. 'I see.'

The tone of her voice was dull, and he continued to look at her some moments more before he said, 'Hasn't anything I've said made any difference? You think I'm lying to you?'

No, she didn't think he was lying. It was something of a revelation, but there was no joy or thankfulness with it. She believed his explanation, but all this had shown her that she wasn't sure of him—or any man's ability to love for ever—deep inside. *The problem wasn't Zac's, it was hers.* She drew in a deep breath, her heart thudding. It had been all along.

Sooner or later something like this would have cropped up and she would have dealt with it in the same way—by running away. And that would have been so much worse if it had been after her child was born, or even after several were born. It was *she* who wasn't cut out for marriage. *Oh, God, help me.* It was a cry from her heart, but one she didn't believe was answerable. She'd destroy them both with her fears if she stayed.

'Tory?' Zac asked tersely. 'Answer me.'

'I don't think you're lying to me.' It was the answer he had wanted but he was in no doubt there was still something terribly wrong. Her face was stricken and as white as a sheet. 'But—' Victoria stopped abruptly. How could she explain?

'But?' He knew he had to keep his temper but it was hard going. She was putting obstacle after obstacle in his way, *their* way.

'But I don't want to be married to you, Zac.' And this time her voice was firmer than it had been for the whole of the conversation, Zac recognised with a sick kind of despair as he forced himself to show no reaction and to keep perfectly calm and still.

'Any particular reason why?' he asked stonily.

'I shouldn't have married you in the first place,' she answered with cruel conviction. 'I see that now, and…and I'm sorry. It's not you—I thought it was, but it's not you. It's me. I can't trust you, Zac; I don't think I'm capable of trusting anybody,' she finished with a bewildered little frown.

'And if I said I could make you trust me?' he asked

with careful control, praying that the tumult of emotion that was tearing him apart wouldn't show in his face. 'What then?'

'Oh, Zac.' It was kind—almost patronising—and for a shocking moment he wanted to shake the truth into her.

'You're saying that's impossible, is that it?' he said with a calm he was far from feeling. 'And you won't give us a chance?'

'Yes.' It was curt and definite.

'I don't accept that for a minute,' he said forcefully.

'Well, whether you accept it or not that's the way I feel,' Victoria said wearily. 'I don't want to keep the baby from you—we can work out access and everything—but I want a divorce. And I'm sorry about today; it should never have happened—'

'The hell it shouldn't,' Zac cut in furiously. 'You're my wife.'

'And it can never happen again,' Victoria finished as though he hadn't spoken. 'Do...do you want me to leave straight away?'

Hell, she meant it. He stared at her, for once in his life utterly lost as to what to do or say next. She loved him, she knew he loved her, and it didn't make any difference. He wished her father wasn't dead so that he could beat him into a pulp. He wished Coral wasn't a woman so he could do the same to her...

'Zac? I can go back to the flat now; I'd be fine there.'

'You're staying here with me until our child is born, Tory.' Suddenly he knew exactly how he was going to handle this. 'And then we'll sort out a place of your own for you and the baby, I promise.' He eyed her white face expressionlessly. 'There'll be no repeat of today, I promise you that too, and no divorce.'

'Zac, I can't stay here after today,' she said tremblingly.

'I'm content with an indefinite separation.' Content? Who was kidding whom? Zac asked himself with savage, caustic self-mockery. 'We can remain friends and bring up the kid amicably—two homes is better than no home at all, after all.'

'But that's not fair on you. Surely a divorce is better?' Victoria asked numbly. 'It would be more straightforward.'

'There has never been a divorce in my family and I don't intend to break the mould,' Zac said shortly. 'I entered this marriage intending it should last our lifetimes; it isn't me who has welched on the deal.' It was below the belt but he was fighting for his life. If he agreed to a divorce he was lost.

Victoria flinched visibly. 'I…I see. I hadn't thought… No, I see.' She nodded miserably. 'If that's what you want.'

'Okay, so that's settled, then.' Zac looked at her tremulous mouth, her white-gold hair that felt like silk and the translucent texture of her skin, and remembered how it had been that day. His arousal was instant and fierce, knotting him up inside as his mind played with the memory of her full rounded stomach and ripe breasts as she had sat astride him, her body joined with his.

He forced himself to rise slowly and walk around the table as though their conversation had been nothing more than pre-dinner banter. 'I'll heat up the food in the microwave,' he said evenly. 'It won't take a minute.'

'I…I don't think I want anything now. I couldn't…'

'You'll eat, Victoria.' Zac's voice was still even, but it carried that certain note she knew meant business. 'And you'll rest, and you'll do all the other things that mean the remainder of this pregnancy will be trouble-free. We're doing right from now on, okay?' She didn't answer right away, and he leant on the table, his eyes fixing on her troubled face as he repeated, 'Okay? I'm taking care of you until the baby is here.'

There was a long, long pause, and then Victoria nodded again as she said, 'I think I would be all right in the flat by myself but if you want me to stay here I will. But just until the baby is born, Zac.' She raised violet-blue eyes to his. 'And then it's back to how things were before the accident.'

Over his dead body. Zac held her gaze, his own straight and clear. 'Of course,' he said silkily.

'And I really think we need to get something in writing,' Victoria said uneasily. 'It needn't be heavy, I don't mean that, but it will make things so much simpler in the long run.'

'You think so?' Zac smiled, a crocodile sort of smile. 'Then your experience of lawyers is different to mine,' he said quietly. 'We can come to some sort of understanding ourselves without involving the vultures. I'll agree to an agreement being drawn up by a third party, something detailing the necessary technicalities, but that's all, Tory. I mean it.'

She stared at him uncertainly. She didn't have a clue where he was coming from, she thought anxiously, but she didn't like it anyway. This smacked of an expensive, beautifully packaged gift that when unwrapped revealed an empty box. But she couldn't fight him now; he was altogether too...too *Zac*.

'And incidentally...' He allowed a tense pause, the black gaze becoming lethal. 'You aren't going to shut me out of my child's life...or yours.'

CHAPTER TEN

THE conversation with Zac had opened up a Pandora's box of issues in her life, Victoria found over the next few weeks, and they were ones which she had mentally brushed under the carpet since childhood without ever really being aware of their existence.

She grappled with them one by one, often trying to push them back inside that box in her head when it got too darn painful, but the lid was well and truly off and she had to acknowledge this was truth time, crucifying as it was.

William had said much the same thing when—as luck would have it—he had called to see her a couple of days after she was on her feet again. She had left a message explaining her changed circumstances on his answering machine the day after Zac had brought her home, along with her new telephone number and a request that he phone her when he could.

Victoria had been in the bath that morning when the phone had rung first thing, and she had nearly fallen off her seat later at breakfast when Zac had said with elaborate casualness, 'Oh, by the way, Howard phoned earlier to see how you were. He's calling by for a cup of coffee later. I didn't think you'd mind.'

'William's coming here?' Victoria stared at the dark face of her husband in amazement. 'To the house?' she added weakly.

'Is anything wrong with that?' Zac asked smoothly.

'No, no, of course not; it's just that...' Victoria didn't know how to say it. 'You don't mind?' she finished tentatively.

'Should I?' The black glittering eyes were piercingly intent.

'Well, you know what I mean.' She wriggled uncomfortably and then stopped abruptly when she realised what she was doing. 'You had the idea at one time we were more than just friends.'

'Victoria, if I thought there was the slightest possibility of anything like that Howard wouldn't get within a mile of you,' Zac said pleasantly, so pleasantly that the portent of his words didn't register for a few seconds. 'However, I am content that as far as you are concerned, at least, the friendship is a platonic one.' He raised dark, sardonic eyebrows at her confusion.

'And you don't mind that William...?' She suddenly realised she had been about to say something stupid and let her voice trail away, conscious of a deep red colour creeping up her neck and into her face. Why couldn't she *think* before she spoke?

'Loves you?' Zac finished evenly, always one to call a spade a spade. He settled back in his chair, narrowing his eyes as his gaze washed over her hot face. 'What do you think, Victoria?' he asked softly. 'Do you think I mind?'

'I don't know.' She didn't know how to handle this conversation either, and it annoyed her. It annoyed her very much.

'William is a rare thing in this world of ours,' Zac said thoughtfully, shifting slightly in his seat so that the powerful muscles in his shoulders bunched under the pale ivory shirt he was wearing and caused her breath to catch in her throat. 'He's an honourable man, or perhaps you didn't know that?'

'Of course I knew,' Victoria snapped testily, irked at the insinuation Zac knew William better than she did. 'I'm just surprised *you* recognised it,' she added waspily.

'I never let prejudice get in the way of discernment,' Zac said evenly. 'You should know that by now.'

'And your discernment picked up William's honourable

qualities immediately, I suppose,' Victoria said irritably. She didn't know if she liked Zac allowing William to visit her, which was quite ridiculous, not to mention perverse.

'More or less.' He tilted his head, inspecting her angry face. 'Of course it was better after I'd met him for a drink and we got down to basics,' he added silkily, his eyes watchful.

'You've gone out for a drink with William?' she asked sharply, her blue eyes flashing to his face. Now she *didn't* like that.

'Uh-huh.' He seemed pleased at her reaction if his lazy—and fascinatingly sexy—smile was anything to go by.

'Why?' she asked brusquely. 'Why on earth would you do that?'

'Because you are my wife, Victoria, and that's my child under your heart.'

She liked the way he put that but she wasn't going to betray it by the flicker of an eyelash. 'That's no answer,' she said militantly. 'And you know that as well as I do.'

'No?' He smiled again but it didn't reach the jet-black eyes. 'I thought it was rather a good one, actually. William Howard cares about you, a blind man could see that, and that's okay—I can live with that—as long as he knows the score.'

'And now you feel he does know the score?' Victoria asked angrily, furious at his arrogance. Megalomaniac—she'd always known it.

'Oh, I'm positive.' He nodded slowly, his eyes cold and hard.

'Well, how cosy.' She didn't really know why she was quite so angry, but it was taking all her will-power not to throw her coffee at him. 'So it's all friends together now, is it?'

He looked at her expressionlessly. 'No, we're not friends, Tory,' he said cryptically, 'and you've still got a hell of a lot to learn about men.'

It was the end of the conversation.

* * *

William was nursing a broken arm when he arrived later that morning—a result of getting a little too close to some trouble on his latest assignment, he told Victoria with a wry smile—and after Mrs Watts, who had shown him into the drawing room, had bustled off to the kitchen for the coffee tray and Victoria had fussed over him he said, 'Well, Blue-eyes, how goes it?'

'Okay.' She smiled brightly, but she had never been able to fool William. 'Zac sends his regards, by the way; he's at work of course—' But she wasn't allowed to get away with the banal.

'Your message said you're back here just until the kid is born?' William, like Zac, didn't waste words. 'You still haven't got things sorted with Zac?' he asked carefully.

'No. Yes. Oh…' She gazed at him helplessly. 'It's such a mess, William. I don't believe Zac was cheating on me, but…'

'Okay.' William settled down in the chair and smiled, his hazel eyes crinkling at the corners. 'Tell Uncle William all about it.' And so she related that last caustic confrontation with Zac almost word for word, but without mentioning the day of lovemaking that had preceded it. That was too precious to share.

'You can't duck and dive, Blue-eyes.' William's face was deadly serious by the time she had finished pouring out her heart. 'The guy loves you, and you love him, and that's his kid you're carrying. You owe it to both of them to make some decisions here.'

Zac and William were more alike than they knew, Victoria thought wryly as William virtually repeated Zac's words.

'You've got to sort these fears out now before they cripple you for life,' William continued softly. 'You do see that, don't you? Take some counselling, do whatever it takes, but get it all out into the open. Then, when you've faced the worst, you can take stock and decide where to

go from there. But it'll be your decision because you know
yourself, and you don't yet.'

It was good advice and Victoria knew it, and they talked
some more before Zac arrived home for an early lunch—
something he had not done before. The two men were cool
with each other, but not unfriendly, although William left
almost immediately.

'You'll let me know when it happens?' William paused
before climbing into the taxi and looked straight at Zac,
who nodded quietly. 'Thanks.' Then, with one last look
at Victoria, he was gone. Victoria watched the taxi depart
feeling more alone than ever.

And so Victoria wrestled with herself. The baby helped.
As the demons of inadequacy, fear, rejection and a whole
host more were brought out into the open, the vigorous
reassurance—as it kicked enough goals to be top of the
first division—from someone who wouldn't be ignored
and was depending on her utterly was like a solid rock
she could hold onto. And hold on she did.

And Zac helped too, strangely enough, as time went on.

She hadn't known what to expect—the first morning
after the cataclysmic day of lovemaking—but he had
metamorphosed into a charming although somewhat remote companion, who treated her as something between
an old friend and maiden aunt, with the emphasis on the
latter.

Not that many maiden aunts had stomachs that were
about to explode, Victoria thought drily as she stood gazing out of the bedroom window one morning in the first
week of December.

It was a bitterly cold day, the sky low and heavy with
grey snow clouds that spoke of severe weather conditions
in the next few days, but Victoria was as warm as toast
as she looked out into the bleak winter's day outside
where the birds were squabbling and fighting over some
bacon rind Mrs Watts had put on the bird table.

She'd had a restless night, partly due to the fact that
she was now as big as a barrage balloon and no matter

how she positioned herself her stomach seemed to be within an inch from her nose, and all her main organs squeezed into some remote painful recess where they didn't fit, but mainly due to a memory that had surfaced the night before and wouldn't leave her alone.

It was her mother who had started the process in a roundabout sort of way by phoning in the afternoon, just before her plane left for the Bahamas, with a duty call wishing her daughter a happy Christmas. She hadn't mentioned Victoria's impending confinement at all until Victoria had brought it up.

'Ah, yes.' Coral's tone had been flat. 'How are things going? I trust you're reconciled to adapting to married life now? I got your note saying you were living with Zac again.'

'I also said it wasn't a permanent situation,' Victoria had reminded her steadily, 'but I felt I ought to let you know in view of the flat being empty for a time. Once the baby's born I shall go back there until Zac sorts out something more suitable.'

'Oh, he's told you, then?' Coral had said without interest.

'Told me?' Victoria had wrinkled her brow at the receiver.

'About the flat,' Coral had snapped irritably. 'I said at the time he might as well, but he was sure you wouldn't live there if you knew. He can be as stubborn as you, Victoria.'

Why did every conversation with her mother resemble a minefield of some kind? Victoria had asked herself wearily, at the same time as her heart began to thud with the uncomfortable feeling Coral knew something she didn't, something important.

'What, exactly, do you mean, Mother?' she'd asked carefully.

There had been a few moments of blank silence, and then Coral had said, her voice tart now, 'Oh, he *hasn't* told you, then? Well, I don't suppose it matters now if you are going to let him buy you a place anyway. The flat was Zac's idea if you must know—there is no friend of mine. Zac didn't want you struggling money-wise or living somewhere unsuitable, so he set it all up with the owner on the understanding you mustn't know. Surely you were *surprised* the rent was so low, Victoria?' she'd added irritably. 'You pay a fraction of the cost. Anyway, I must go. I'll speak to you when I return in January.'

Victoria had sat in stunned disbelief, holding the phone for a good five minutes after it had gone dead, but no matter how she'd tried to explain it away one fact remained. He had been worried about her, so worried he had smoothed the way by the only avenue left open to him. Oh, Zac, Zac... She'd felt more confused than ever.

She had made the excuse of feeling tired—which wasn't really an excuse at all as she was constantly exhausted these days due to one sleepless night after another—when Zac had arrived home later, and had gone to bed without telling him about her mother's phone call. She'd needed to think about this, digest it, before she discussed it with him. Everything was getting more and more complicated.

And then, as she had lain staring into the darkness with sleep a million miles away, the memory had come to haunt her.

It had featured her father and Linda Ward and herself. She could only have been four or five, and there was a garden party going on. She was sitting in one of those upholstered sofa swings on Linda's lap, and her father had joined them. From that point it was blurred, but her father must have been short with her because she recalled Linda saying that she—Victoria—was the innocent one in all of this, and it wasn't fair to take it all out on a child.

And her father had cried. That was the thing she had buried, because she hadn't been able to cope with it at the time—she had been too unused to any show of emotion. But he had definitely cried.

The phone ringing at the side of her now interrupted further reminiscences, and she picked it up quickly, glad to come out of the misty shadows that puzzled and confused her.

'Tory?' Zac's voice was dark and gentle, and she shivered deep inside. 'How are you feeling?' he asked softly.

'Feeling?' she echoed dazedly, her mind a million miles away.

'You felt off colour last night, and you had backache this morning at breakfast,' Zac reminded her quietly. 'Is everything okay?'

'Oh, that—oh, no, I'm fine,' Victoria said hastily. Fine. What a stupid word, she thought with savage self-deprecation. She wasn't fine; she was anything but fine. She missed him. He was living in the same house, eating his meals with her, talking to her about his work, his interests, *everything* these days, and the more he did that, the further away he seemed to get. Because it made her realise what she was missing. Oh, she was a mess...

'The weather forecast is foul, so just put your feet up today,' Zac said softly, 'and if your back is still troubling you when I come home I'll give you a massage.'

A massage? Victoria remembered how he had looked at breakfast that morning, his lean, muscled body clothed in a designer suit and light blue shirt, black hair slicked back from his forehead and his tanned skin carrying a deliciously clean, lemony smell that carried undertones of raw male. It had taken her a full hour to recover. And he was talking about a massage...

'It's...it's all right,' she said in a flustered gasp. 'I...I'm sure I'll be—'

'Fine?' he finished lazily. 'Well, we'll see. Goodbye for now.'

How would Linda react if she went to see her? Alone with her thoughts again, Victoria returned to a safer topic than Zac. The baby was due in another three weeks so if she was going to go now was the time. But perhaps her father's mistress wouldn't want to see the daughter of her old lover? If she was at home, that was.

Linda was at home, and she welcomed Victoria with a warmth that surprised the younger woman as she said, 'How lovely to see you.' Linda's looks, although pleasant, had never been stunning, and now Victoria saw the older woman had obviously decided to ride the passing years gracefully. Her make-up was perfect but discreet, and her thick hair cut expensively well but showing liberal amounts of silver among the brown. 'I'd heard the baby was expected soon, and I've been looking in the paper every night for the last week or so to see if it's arrived,' Linda said with her gentle smile.

'Have you?' Victoria was surprised but rather pleased.

Once Linda had led her into the sitting room—a cosy room Victoria remembered vaguely from the past, with good but slightly shabby furniture enhanced by a roaring log fire in front of which the most enormous tabby cat lay—Victoria knew she had to speak quickly before she lost her nerve.

'You'll probably think I'm being silly,' she began hesitantly, 'and I hope you won't mind what I'm about to say, but it is important. My mother told me some months ago about you and...and my father.' She was blushing furiously but she couldn't help it.

Linda's face straightened but her eyes were steady as she said, 'I've nothing to hide, Victoria. What do you want to know?'

'I don't understand half of it, and it's none of my business, I know that, but something has been bothering me.' Oh, this was difficult, awful. She should never have come.

And then Linda made everything easier as she leant forward, her eyes soft, and said, 'Of course it's your business, Victoria.'

It was simple from then on, and after Victoria had finished speaking Linda was quiet for a full minute before she said, 'I'll make some tea and then we'll talk properly.'

They talked until lunchtime, and when Linda asked her to stay and share a meal Victoria promptly accepted. She was so glad she had come; she had learnt so much.

Linda's face had glowed as she had talked of Victoria's father. 'We met just a year too late,' she said softly. 'His marriage with your mother was virtually an arranged one—two families who had known each other for years wanting their offspring to wed. Your father had never met anyone he really cared about, and your mother was very attractive, so he let himself be talked into it. He knew from his honeymoon it was a terrible mistake, but you were conceived almost straight away. We met a few months later.'

Linda's hand went out to hold Victoria's as she continued, 'Your mother…well, she didn't plan on having a baby, and your father always said it was a miracle you were conceived anyway. She didn't like the intimate side of marriage at all. But there it was; you were on your way and neither of us felt it was right for him to leave until you were older.'

'He stayed because of me?' Victoria asked slowly. 'But he never took any interest in me, not really,' she added bewilderedly.

'He wanted to, but your mother was very clever in using any weakness as a weapon,' Linda said a trifle bitterly. 'Added to which he wasn't a man who could show affection easily, and he was consumed by guilt most of the time. He felt he was being unfair to you, to me, and, of course, to your mother. I finished with him several times—for his sake, not mine,' Linda added quickly, 'but we couldn't live without each other; it was as simple as that. And Coral didn't actually mind.' Linda's voice reflected her amazement. 'As long as he remained her husband in name and allowed her to live as she chose. In fact, she almost encouraged our liaison.'

'I know.' Victoria nodded, remembering all her mother had said.

'Once Coral had sent you away to school he spent most of his time here,' Linda said quietly. 'And then…he was gone, along with all the plans we had made for the future.'

'And you've never met anyone else?' Victoria asked slowly, her heart going out to the gentle, softly spoken woman in front of her who was the very antithesis of Coral.

'I've never wanted to.' Linda smiled a sad smile. 'He was the only one for me, and I know I was the only one for him. We were utterly faithful to each other. It happens like that sometimes.'

'It happens like that sometimes.'

The first lazy fat snowflakes were beginning to fall out of the laden sky as Victoria waved goodbye to Linda later that afternoon and stepped into the taxi the other woman had ordered for her, her head spinning with all she had been told.

'It happens like that sometimes.' She couldn't get the refrain out of her head. She felt as emotionally drained as if she had been caught up in some terrible tragedy, but then she had in a way, she told herself silently as the taxi sped along the fast whitening roads. An old tragedy, but a tragedy nevertheless, which had affected everyone who'd played a part. Her father's entrapment in a loveless marriage and his ongoing guilt and pain and confusion had touched all of them, but most of all her, as she had struggled to make sense of an adult world she couldn't comprehend. But that was the past, and she understood better now…

The niggling ache in the small of her back that had started first thing that morning was getting worse, along with the snow which was now coming down in a feathery white curtain. It was beautiful, Victoria thought wonderingly. And life was beautiful—it was. And she didn't want to miss out on it. Her father *had* been capable of love; in his own way he had been faithful to Linda from the moment he met her because he *loved* her. His mistake had been in marrying the wrong woman, she realised with a thudding heart.

And had she married the wrong man?

The taxi driver swore as two small children muffled up to the eyeballs threw a snowball at his cab, but Victoria didn't even hear him, a missile of gigantic proportions crashing into her consciousness. *Zac was her 'sometimes'.*

She loved Zac with all her heart, and she believed he loved her in the same way. Her father, cold and remote as he had been, had loved Linda Ward almost to the exclusion of anything—or anyone—else, his frustration at not being able to live with the woman he loved gnawing away at him until he had died prematurely. He hadn't played the field, he hadn't gone from one affair to another...

Zac had wanted to take care of her all along, even when she had rejected him for the second time. He had been prepared to wait for her, playing a part in her life and his child's until she grew to trust him; she saw that now. *She saw it.*

Or was she fooling herself because she so wanted to believe what her heart was telling her? Her stomach turned over and all the old doubts reared their heads before she took a deep breath, staring out of the car window at the thick curtain of snow falling from a white-grey sky, the faint golden glow from the streetlamps barely making an impression in the fading light.

She loved Zac. She was her father's daughter, not her mother's, and she loved him. Her father had made a terrible mistake in marrying the wrong woman, but her mistake would be a hundred times worse than that if she let the right man go because of her cowardice. And that was what it boiled down to. She was frightened of opening the door and allowing Zac free entry, frightened of the power it would give him and her own vulnerability. But if he loved her as she loved him he was in the same position, wasn't he? It worked both ways. There was no get-out clause.

She continued to chew at the dilemma all the way home, shifting in her seat as the ache in her back grew more uncomfortable and began to make her feel slightly nauseous.

It was just after four when the taxi drew into the drive, and before it had even drawn to a halt Zac was there, his face thunderous as he wrenched open the door. 'Where the hell have you been?' She couldn't remember ever seeing him so angry. 'Where the *hell* have you been?' he repeated furiously, his eyes flashing.

'I've been to see someone.' Victoria stared at her husband in amazement. 'What on earth is the matter?'

'I popped home lunchtime to see how you were,' he bit out savagely, 'and Mrs Watts didn't have a clue where you were.'

'You popped home...' And then she recalled his telephone call earlier that day, and immediately felt horribly guilty. 'But you said you wouldn't be home till five. Oh, I'm sorry, Zac, really.'

As the taxi driver joined Zac on the drive and received a ferocious glare for his pains, he clearly thought he ought to make his position clear. 'Nothin' to do with me, mate,' he said cheerily, 'although I thought it was a bit strange she was gallivantin' on a day like this in her condition. Still, that's women for you. My missus is the same.'

Zac wasn't interested in the taxi driver's 'missus' and said so, softening his testiness with a handsome tip that sent the man away happy with a merry toot of his horn.

He said not another word as he helped Victoria over the snow and into the house, but immediately he closed the front door behind them his simmering rage bubbled over again.

'I've called everyone we know—and the hospital—

since lunchtime,' he said tightly. 'I've even had William phoning round.'

'William?'

She stared at him in amazement, and his snarl of, 'Yes, William,' was not reassuring as he took her elbow and steered her into the drawing room, his face still dark with temper.

'I called to see if you'd gone round there, and he thought he might know a few folk I didn't,' Zac said in a low sort of growl. 'The guy was as worried as me, so you'd better call him in a minute and put his mind at ease.'

'I will.' He *must* have been worried to ask for William's help.

'But not before you tell me what was so important that you high-tail it on a day like this,' he grated.

There was a strange kind of tightening in her stomach, but it barely registered on Victoria's consciousness as she sought for words to explain why it had been so important to see Linda that day. She just didn't know where to start, she thought helplessly.

'I...I had to see someone,' she said at last.

'Male or female?' It was a gruff bark, and she suddenly realised that along with his unquestionable worry there had been an element of something else—confusion, doubt, even jealousy?

She stared at him in absolute amazement. 'Zac, I'm as big as a house,' she said blankly. 'You didn't think...?'

'I didn't know what to think,' he prevaricated angrily, but she had seen the look of fierce relief in his eyes before he could veil his glance, and it wrenched her heart. They were stupid—the pair of them, they were stupid, she thought tremblingly, before she qualified that with, But it's my fault. He doesn't know where he stands or what to think.

'I went to see my father's mistress.' She sat down in one of the big soft easy chairs in front of the fire as she spoke; she was really feeling quite odd. 'There were things

I had to ask her, things I needed to know. Zac, they loved each other. I mean they *really* loved each other, like…like us.'

'Us?' He had gone very still.

'I've been so stupid.' Tears pricked at her eyes but she blinked them away determinedly. She had to say it all; she couldn't break down now. 'I know that now. Because I do love you, more than anything else in all the world, and I can't live without you, Zac. I don't want to stay in a separate house to you, or for our child to divide its time between us. I…I know about the flat, about you paying for it for me—' And then, as the emotion she had felt when Coral had first told her overwhelmed her in a torrent of love and thankfulness and joy, her voice broke.

'Tory?' And then he was kneeling at her side, and kissing her in a way that took no account of her size, his voice incoherent as he punctuated the kisses with wild, tender murmurings until both their faces were damp, their tears mingling.

'Don't ever leave me again, Tory.' He drew back at last, his eyes naked with the agony he had felt then. 'I couldn't go through that again and remain sane.'

'I won't, I won't.' She traced the contours of his face with wondering hands, amazed at the release of contentment and peace that flooded her. 'Whatever happens in the future, whatever problems we have to face, we'll see them through together. I promise. No more running away. I know who I am now, Zac, for the first time ever.'

'There'll only ever be you, you know that, don't you?' Zac said softly, placing his hands over hers as she cupped his strong face in her fingers. 'You're everything to me, Tory. You have been from the first moment I laid eyes on you.'

'I know.' She smiled mistily. 'I really do know now.'

'Children will be wonderful, gifts from God, but if it had only been me and you to the end of our days that would have been enough for me.' He took her in his arms again, kissing her passionately as he remained kneeling at her side. 'I was determined I would wait for as long as it took to get you to believe in me; I had enough love for both of us. I would never have let you go,' he said with a fierce resolve that thrilled her.

'I know that too.' Her voice was faintly teasing as she added, 'No divorce, remember? The Harding name must not be soiled.'

'Ah...' His eyes narrowed slightly, his mouth twisting with wry humour. 'I have a slight confession to make there. There *has* been a divorce in the illustrious Harding ancestry, more than one in fact. But it was the only thing I could think of at the time.'

'Shame on you, Zac Harding,' Victoria said reprovingly.

'I never said I fight fair.' He smiled sexily. 'But I wanted to keep time on my side. I didn't have much else going for me.'

'Talking of time...' Victoria looked straight into his eyes, relishing the moment. 'That backache wasn't just backache. I'm sitting in a wet chair.'

'A wet...?'

She saw the dawning realisation in his face even before she said, her voice serene, 'The baby is on its way, Zac. My waters have broken.'

CHAPTER ELEVEN

THE snow was inches thick when they stepped out into a transformed landscape of ethereal beauty some minutes later, but the tranquillity of the moment was quite ruined by Zac's loud and profuse swearing as he surveyed the blocked drive.

'It will be all right, don't worry.' Victoria smiled at him—loving him, needing him—but then, as the mild backache she had been experiencing all day switched to her stomach with dramatic intensity, inflicting the sort of pain she wouldn't wish on her worst enemy, she almost doubled up on the doorstep.

'*Tory?* Hell, Tory, what is it? What's happening?'

He was panicking. That thought registered through the overwhelming pain, and then, as the contraction subsided, she raised her head and looked into the horrified face of her husband. Although it didn't look like Zac. In fact she didn't think she had ever seen such sheer terror on a human face before. And then she realised. *His mother.* His mother had died giving birth to his little sister when he was ten years old, and at ten you could take in quite a lot. And it had been an early birth—like this one. He had his own wounds from the past that needed healing.

'I'm okay, this is perfectly natural.' She managed a fairly normal smile. 'You clear the drive so we can get out onto the main road; there's plenty of time.' *Please, God, let there be plenty of time,* she added in silent supplication.

'Sit in the car.' His voice was shaking but his face was Zac's again, and once he had established her in the front seat, draped in a blanket, she watched him clearing the drive like a man possessed as shovels of snow went in all directions.

The next contraction hit after only four minutes, and it took all Victoria's will-power to sit quietly and do her breathing exercises, rather than opening the car door and yelling for him to be quick. She was frightened and she wanted the safe, reassuring solidity of the hospital more than she would have thought possible.

Once they were on the road, the windscreen-wipers labouring under the inordinate volume of soft, exquisitely beautiful crystals that had suddenly become such an enemy, they travelled at a snail's pace through the choked streets of the capital, passing other intrepid Londoners who were determined to do battle with the elements. Stranded cars were everywhere, although the roads became a little better as they neared the hospital.

'A little bit of snow and England stops.' Zac was directing his fear and anxiety at the weather, scowling ferociously at the vista beyond the windscreen, and suddenly Victoria saw the funny side of it. Needless to say she was between pains.

'This will be one to tell the grandchildren.' They were only a couple of streets away now and everything was all right again. 'Of course we could cap it by my giving birth here in the car. That would make a really good story, don't you think?'

'Don't.' It was weak but he managed a grin—he could see the lights of the hospital and he'd carry her from here if he had to.

Once Zac had pulled up outside the maternity wing he insisted, much to Victoria's mortification, on fetching a wheelchair and wheeling her into the warm, antiseptic surrounds with the sort of ceremony normally accorded to royalty. She felt utterly ridiculous, but then another contraction gripped her—they were coming every three minutes now—and she couldn't have cared less if she had been on a handcart.

Once the hospital machine took over it went like clock-work, and within minutes Victoria was established in a fairly innocuous delivery room, with a gowned Zac at the side of her—she was sure he was the only man in the world who could wear such a garment and still look devastating—and a plump, motherly midwife peering between her legs and beaming happily.

'You *have* been busy, Mrs Harding.' The soft Irish brogue was full of approval, and Victoria and Zac exchanged a weak grin. 'Not long to go now,' she added reassuringly. 'You're doing fine.'

'Not long' was relative. At the end of another three hours Victoria was ready to take a vow of celibacy, but then, just when she had decided enough was enough and with the next pain she was going to bellow like the woman next door, who had deafened them all with her trumpetings for the last hour, she knew she wanted to push. She'd never felt so glad about anything in her life.

Zac wouldn't have believed the strength in Victoria's grasp if he hadn't felt it as she gripped his hand, but in view of the pain she had gone through he felt his crushed fingers were the least he could do. Everyone seemed to know what they were doing, Victoria most of all, and he was finding the deeply rooted fear and panic—hitherto barely acknowledged even by himself, but which had been with him since he was ten years old and felt his world fall apart—were swallowed up by the sheer wonder of what was unfolding in front of him.

At ten minutes past nine everything seemed to happen very quickly. Victoria gave one last enormous push, and instead of the slow sliding out Zac had expected his son shot out into the world with all the force of a true Harding. And he was huge. Big hands, big feet, and with a shock of curly black hair that made him look weeks old instead of newborn as he peered up at his father with dark eyes and a surprised expression.

'It's a boy, Tory.' There was a note in Zac's voice that

caused the midwife—blasé as she was by now—to blink away the tears and swallow hard as she cut the cord and wrapped the baby in a blanket, handing him to Victoria just as he was with the smears of birth still on him, and his damp hair in tight little curls.

'Hello, Sweet-pea.' As Victoria stared down into the tiny, screwed-up face that nevertheless looked ridiculously like Zac's, the baby blinked and yawned widely, looking back at her with something approaching astonishment as though to say, How on earth did I get here and don't I know you?

And then Zac held him, reducing Victoria to tears, before a nurse weighed and checked him while the midwife saw to Victoria.

'He's a ten-pounder.' The nurse was young and sounded quite awestricken as she looked at Victoria's slight frame. 'Ten pounds, three ounces, and he's twenty-three inches long.'

'And Mum doesn't need a single stitch, not one,' the midwife said approvingly. She obviously considered that Victoria was her star pupil. 'You're made for child-bearing inside, love.'

'Am I?' Victoria was inordinately pleased.

'What are you going to call him?' the nurse asked enquiringly as she wrote a tiny label to be attached to the baby's ankle.

'James Zachary.' Victoria smiled at Zac as she spoke. James had been her father's name and one of the possibles for a boy, although they hadn't finally decided. But it seemed right now.

And then James Zachary was in Victoria's arms again and the hospital staff bustled away with promises of returning in a few minutes with two cups of tea.

'He's beautiful, Tory.' Zac was sitting on the bed with his arm cradling Victoria as his other hand stroked the tiny face. 'Thank you, my love. Thank you.'

'I love you.' Victoria smiled up at him, her heart in her

eyes. 'I love you so much.' And there was no reservation left, no fear, just a love that soared into the heavens and anticipated the years ahead with pure joy. They would create their own family, she and Zac, she thought jubilantly. A family where their children would always know they were loved and wanted, precious products of their parents' deep love.

'And I love you,' Zac returned huskily, looking at the perfect picture his wife and son made and wondering if any man had ever felt as blessed as he did, and also if it was quite right for him to be feeling such consuming desire for Victoria right at that moment.

He bent his dark head and kissed her, and Victoria kissed him back passionately, their son cradled between them. They had wasted enough time with their legacies from the past, Victoria thought fleetingly. She was free from her self-doubts and fears now, and with love and understanding she would teach Zac he didn't have to try and make it on his own any more—that he could share everything with her because she was the other part of him, his soulmate. And she knew he would embrace the concept whole-heartedly; already, over the past few weeks, he had talked to her and communicated his innermost thoughts like never before. The future was theirs, *theirs*, and it was going to be glorious.

And when the door opened a few minutes later, and the nurse's bright voice said, 'Here's that tea to perk you up,' neither of them heard her.

EXPECTING

She's sexy, she's successful... and she's pregnant!

Relax and enjoy these new stories about spirited women and gorgeous men, whose passion results in pregnancies... sometimes unexpectedly! All the new parents-to-be will discover that the business of making babies brings with it the most special love of all....

Harlequin Presents® brings you one **EXPECTING!** book each month throughout 1999.
Look out for:

The Baby Secret by Helen Brooks
Harlequin Presents #2004, January 1999

Expectant Mistress by Sara Wood
Harlequin Presents #2010, February 1999

Dante's Twins by Catherine Spencer
Harlequin Presents #2016, March 1999

Available at your favorite retail outlet.

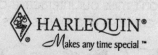

HARLEQUIN®
Makes any time special ™

Sexy, desirable and...a daddy?

THE AUSTRALIANS

Stories of romance Australian-style, guaranteed to fulfill that sense of adventure!

This February 1999 look for

Baby Down Under

by **Ann Charlton**

Riley Templeton was a hotshot Queensland lawyer with a reputation for ruthlessness and a weakness for curvaceous blondes. Alexandra Page was everything that Riley *wasn't* looking for in a woman, but when she finds a baby on her doorstep that leads her to the dashing lawyer, he begins to see the virtues of brunettes—and babies!

The Wonder from Down Under: where spirited women win the hearts of Australia's most independent men!

Available February 1999
at your favorite retail outlet.

HARLEQUIN®
Makes any time special ™

HARLEQUIN ❖ PRESENTS®

WANTED: ONE WEDDING DRESS

A trilogy by
Sharon Kendrick

Three brides in search of the perfect dress—and the perfect husband!

In February 1999 wedding-dress designer
Holly Lovelace marries the man of her dreams in
One Bridegroom Required!
Harlequin Presents® #2011

In March 1999 Amber has her big day in
One Wedding Required!
Harlequin Presents® #2017

In April 1999 Ursula, Amber's sister,
walks up the aisle, too!
One Husband Required!
Harlequin Presents® #2023

Available wherever Harlequin books are sold.

❖ HARLEQUIN®
Makes any time special ™

Coming Next Month

HARLEQUIN PRESENTS®

THE BEST HAS JUST GOTTEN BETTER!